Shifting Sands Resort

This is the first book of the Shifting Sands Resort series. All of my books are standalones (No cliffhangers! Always a happy ending!) and can be read independently, but many of these characters reappear in subsequent books, and there is a complete series arc, so you may enjoy reading these books in order:

Tropical Tiger Spy (Book 1)
Tropical Wounded Wolf (Book 2)
Tropical Bartender Bear (Book 3)
Tropical Lynx's Lover (Book 4)
Tropical Dragon Diver (Book 5)
Tropical Panther's Penance (Book 6)
Tropical Christmas Stag (Book 7)
Tropical Leopard's Longing (Book 8)
Tropical Lion's Legacy (Book 9)
Tropical Dragon's Destiny (Book 10)

The Master Shark's Mate (A Fire & Rescue Shifters/Shifting Sands Resort crossover, occurs in the timeline between *Tropical Wounded Wolf* and *Tropical Bartender Bear*)

Firefighter Phoenix (A Fire & Rescue Shifters novel, has scenes set at Shifting Sands Resort, and occurs in the timeline between *Tropical Christmas Stag* and *Tropical Leopard's Longing*)

1

Prologue

SNOW FLEW BENEATH RUNNING tiger paws; the time for stealth was long past and Tony flat out ran, the precious drive carefully held between his teeth.

Behind him, there was distant shouting in Russian and a spatter of gunfire. Bullets struck stone around him.

Tony zigzagged a few paces, then sprang for the nearest wall. It would have been an impossible jump as a man, nearly nine feet in the air, but as a tiger he cleared it easily and landed in the deep snowbank beyond with an explosion of snow.

See, his tiger said smugly. *We got out easily!*

Concentrate on staying *free*, Tony reminded him. *Gloat later.*

Running through loose powder was harder than using the cleared road, but his pursuers would have considerably more trouble following him off-road. Down the mountain they ran, springing through the snow straight for the forest below.

Keen tiger ears heard the roar of snowmobiles starting pursuit from the compound; his lead was not a comfortable one.

Tigers were not built for marathon running, but just as Tony's inner tiger gave his human form certain advantages of strength and perception, his human could give his tiger endurance. Together, they were able to make it down into the cover of the trees before the machines could close the distance behind them.

Don't bite down, don't bite down, Tony reminded himself in a loop, trying not to drool too badly around the drive as he leaped over fallen logs and sprinted for the helicopter coordinates.

Please be undiscovered, he begged briefly.

But he had no such luck. The pilot was gone, and a handful of guards were milling about the snowy clearing. Tony spat the drive out; he'd need his teeth for this.

Teegr? A guard was saying in Russian into a staticky radio with confusion.

Their warning was too late.

Tony slammed into the man, driving him face-first into the packed snow. The impact knocked him out and Tony spun to face the others. One dropped his gun in alarm and sank to his knees, and two of them simply fled. Tony charged the only guard who remained armed and wrestled the gun from his hands with teeth and claws.

The snarling surprise attack was enough to drive them from the clearing but Tony knew it wouldn't be long before they regrouped and reinforcements from the mountain compound joined them. He shifted back to human and fished around in the snow desperately for the drive, naked and shivering.

He frowned when he finally found it; he'd managed to put divots in the casing with his teeth, but they weren't deep. Hopefully the moisture from the snow and saliva wouldn't damage the information.

He tossed the drive into the seat of the helicopter and began the process of spooling up the engines, pulling a frigid insulated coverall over his freezing body.

The blades began to turn, and Tony crammed his numb feet into stiff boots that were a size too small and as cold as the coveralls. His hands were too cramped and painful to tie them, so he didn't bother, closing the helicopter door and pulling the headset over his head. His frozen ears protested and he turned the radio on and dialed it to the right frequency.

"Tiger One, this is Tiger One to Castle," he said.

The blades were almost up to speed, and the trees around the clearing were beginning to whip around in their draft, snow whirling.

"Tiger One, this is Castle, what's your status?"

Rick's voice had never sounded so welcome.

"My status is really fucking cold," Tony said sharply, blowing on his tingling fingers. "Leaving Base One now. I've got the Prize." He eyed the drive and hoped again that his teeth hadn't damaged it beyond repair.

A shot left a round dimple on the windshield surrounded by a spiderweb.

"Okay, make that hot," Tony amended. He fingered the controls and the helicopter rose rapidly into the air as more shots followed. "Mind if I put you on hold while I'm being shot at?"

The forest shrank beneath him as the machine lifted into the air and Tony piloted away down the valley. He didn't dare breathe until the clearing was behind him, and the forest itself was a model train vista dusted with fake snow. None of the shots seemed to have caused major damage; the helicopter remained responsive and the fuel levels looked good. He swung towards the looming Siberian mountains in the south and thumbed the radio back on.

"Everything grrrreeeeeat?" Rick casually asked.

Through his chattering teeth, Tony managed to say, "Except for the impending hypothermia and the frostbit fingers."

"If Rochelle gets the information off that drive that we think is there, it will be worth a few fingers," Rick assured him.

"I hope it helps," Tony agreed, searching for mittens in the emergency gear. "But promise me one thing."

"Anything you want," Rick said confidently.

"The next assignment is somewhere *warm*. Somewhere I can have testicles again." The coveralls hadn't warmed up much and every inch of his skin was protesting the cold contact.

Rick laughed. "I've got just the job. You're going to love it."

Chapter 1

AMBER ALLEN LEANED out the open window of the resort van and drew in a breath of the fragrant jungle air. She could identify most of the plants by sight, but scents couldn't be conveyed in textbooks.

"Mr. Big owns the whole island," Jimmy, the scruffy man who had met her at the airport, shouted over the sound of the engine and crashing waves. "About a quarter of it was developed for the resort in the eighties, and his estate takes up another quarter of it. If you're lucky, you might get a tour."

He gave Amber a sleazy smile over his shoulder, suggesting that he personally could get her just such a treat. "The rest is left natural jungle, except the airstrip you came in on."

Amber wanted to ask if the island owner's name was really Mr. Big, but loathed the idea of encouraging Jimmy to keep talking. She had already made the mistake of mentioning her love of plants in a conversational way, and Jimmy had taken it as if she had batted her eyelashes and asked him to tell her *everything*.

He made another hairpin turn around a switchback with a steep cliff on one side, barely shrouded in trailing greenery, and a rocky plunge to the ocean on the other. The road was scarcely wide enough for the rusty van and had potholes large enough to swallow a bus.

"Scarlet took over the resort about three years back," Jimmy continued, as if Amber weren't studiously ignoring him to concentrate on staying in her seat. "She cleaned up the old cottages right nice and made it a shifters-only haven. We get animal folk from all over now. We've got a British boar couple, and a chinchilla from Singapore. There's a Siberian tiger, but I'd guess he's from the East Coast by his accent, not Siberia. Russian name, though."

Amber flinched despite herself and looked up in alarm. She wasn't sure she could get used to the idea of a place where she could speak freely about being a shifter.

"You didn't say what kind of shifter you were," Jimmy said invitingly, meeting her eyes in the mirror.

"A cat," Amber said vaguely, glad when he had to break their eye contact to navigate the narrow, bumpy road.

"Here kitty, kitty," Jimmy laughed, and Amber forced a smile, though she found it nothing but creepy. "How'd you hear about us?"

"I found out about it from my roommate," Amber said reluctantly, clinging to her armrest and her bag as the van whipped around another blind corner. None of the seat belts worked, and she was beginning to wish that she had more strenuously resisted her roommate Alice's suggestion that a tropical vacation was just what she needed. At least she should have insisted on something more traditional when her friend had encouraged this rather peculiar destination.

"That's usually how it is," Jimmy said sagely. "Can't exactly take an ad out in an airline magazine, you know, but word of mouth serves us well."

Miraculously, the road straightened, widened, and then opened out into a gorgeous verdant lawn, with lush landscaping peppered with low walls of dark volcanic rock and brilliantly flowering bushes. A tasteful sign announced, "Shifting Sands Island Resort." Below, it emphasized, "Private Property. Residents Only. No trespassing. No hunting."

"Here we go!" Jimmy pulled up to a wall that Amber realized after a moment was actually a building, with a tile roof almost completely hidden in thick greenery.

There was no actual door into the building, just an open arch that went down a few steps into a little covered porch, which in turn opened into a charming little courtyard with a fountain and pots of plants everywhere. Amber couldn't stop herself from carefully touching spiky blossoms and stroking the green pitchers. There were orchids and hydrangeas and passion flowers. She paused at a brilliant red flower and frowned at its colorful leaves.

"The courtyard is the only place we will grow this kind of ginger," a voice behind her said. "It's a very popular ornamental on the mainland, but is very invasive and is choking out the native ginger strain there. Even in pots, we protect it from the wind to keep it from seeding out."

"I've read about the problems they're having with it in Hawaii," Amber said, turning to face the voice.

"You'd have to talk to our gardener, Graham, about that," the woman said dismissively. "I'm Scarlet."

She had hair as vivid as the ginger back in a neat bun, a shade that was more likely to be dyed than natural, but it matched her coloring perfectly. Her skin was unexpectedly pale for the latitude, and her eyes were flinty emerald green. Amber couldn't decide if she was very old, or very young—she could have been either. She wore tailored khaki pants and a spotless white blouse. Everything about her said 'no nonsense,' right down to her perfectly shaped nails, showing just a hint of subtle shine.

"Do you have more bags, Ms. Allen?" Scarlet asked.

"Ah, no," Amber said, keenly aware of her travel-wrinkled clothes and the chips in the bright nail polish she had impulsively applied before leaving home. "I decided to travel with just carry-ons."

That earned her a brief smile of approval. "A wise decision," Scarlet said mildly, turning to lead Amber through another archway. "Shifting Sands supplies the finest in all the consumables you should need, we have complete laundry facilities, and the clothing-optional setting means you need very little. Please don't hesitate to let the staff know if you find that there is anything you need."

The room Amber was led into was clearly an office, with an actual door, and a desk and a tidy bookcase. Windows beyond the desk looked down over the jungle, and Amber caught a glimpse of ocean before sitting in the chair she was gestured to.

"There are a few ground rules I need to clarify with you," Scarlet said, and Amber felt as if she had just been called into the principal's office. "Our first rule is no predation."

Amber blinked. "Excuse me?"

"There is no hunting permitted anywhere on the grounds. We have shifters of all types, and the island is home to several native endangered species. This restriction includes rodents, lizards, and birds, as well as larger mammals. Do you agree to these terms?" Scarlet's green eyes drilled into Amber.

"I, ah, yes, of course."

"If you would like to go fishing, we have equipment that can be checked out at the beachhouse, and expeditions can be arranged if there is enough interest. You are also welcome to fish in animal form." Scarlet opened a folder. Amber recognized the paperwork she had nervously filled out online. "We can skip the grazing restrictions, of course."

"As long as there are no catnip beds I need to stay out of," Amber giggled then stilled at Scarlet's withering stare. "Of course," she said contritely.

"You didn't specify what kind of cat you are," Scarlet said, pen poised over the paper. "Domestic, or...?"

Amber swallowed. "Andean mountain cat."

Scarlet raised one eyebrow. "I've never met one of those before," she said thoughtfully.

The tiny hope that Amber had been trying not to nurse turned to ash in her chest.

Apparently not noticing, Scarlet wrote neatly on the form, then turned it to Amber. "Please initial."

Amber did, numbly.

Scarlet took the form back. "There is no food storage in your cottage. We are in the tropics, and insects and other pests are quickly attracted to any unattended food and trash. You are welcome to eat at the dining hall buffet at any time of day, and there is a limited menu available at the bar during their open hours as well."

Scarlet passed a contract over the desk. "Please sign here to indicate your agreement with our rules."

Amber obediently signed two copies of that, and four more similar forms regarding medical care, liability, a draconian privacy policy, and a contract for payment.

Then Scarlet was all polite smiles, rising and giving Amber a firm handshake. "Your application suggested that you would prefer privacy over beach immediacy, so I've assigned you cottage twenty-seven in the upper ring." She handed Amber a glossy pamphlet that unfolded to a map, and circled the cottage in question, well away from any neighbors, and gave her the key.

"That looks great," Amber said with a nod.

"This is the dining hall." Scarlet pointed to the long building just below the office. "Though the drinks and buffet are available at all times, meal times are well worth making the effort to attend; our chef is incomparable. Massages and grooming services can be scheduled at the spa. There are yoga, dance, and meditation sessions daily at the event hall. We have a semi-formal dance on Saturday evening, you are welcome to attend."

Scarlet showed Amber where the schedules were printed in the pamphlet, pointed out a few of the other features, and gave her copies of the paperwork with a clear air of dismissal. "*Pura vida,*" she said off-handedly.

Pure life was the motto of Costa Rica, and seemed to be used as hello and goodbye, as well.

Amber stood for a long moment outside of Scarlet's door, clutching her carry-ons. Then she oriented her map and found her way out of the courtyard and down into the gleaming resort.

Chapter 2

TONY LUKIN WAS NOT good at pretending to relax, and he was beginning to regret his request to Rick for a warm assignment without specifying 'and also not incredibly tedious.'

He scowled across the beach to the ocean, waiting for it to do anything but splash on the shore in regular intervals.

The most exciting thing it had done in the hour he'd been out here was attract a few birds, which had circled him hoping for food and then left. The miniature crabs that dug little holes and scuttled around moving sand piles had entertained him for about a minute on the first day. Beach-combing had turned up a lot of broken shells and lackluster pebbles.

He'd tried three different books of varying fluff, he'd tried closing his eyes for a nap, he'd even gone for a swim, in both human and tiger form.

And the sum of it was, vacation bored him.

Vacation that was just a sham bored him even more.

He wanted to be doing *something*, and it grated on his nerves that he wasn't. He'd been at Shifting Sands for a full week by now, and he was no closer to uncovering what he'd come to find than he had been when he stepped off the plane.

Tony growled, and rolled out of the beach chair, wrapping the towel around his waist. He'd become used to walking around without any covering, and it certainly simplified shifting, but he was still more than a little concerned about sunburning his more delicate parts.

There was an easy set of stairs up to the pool, where tables with umbrellas and lounge chairs were about a quarter full of guests in various stages of allowing sun on their skin.

He dropped himself easily beside a woman sunbathing alone in a generous spotted bikini that left acres of skin exposed. She spilled out over her lounge chair, and it groaned beneath her weight as she shifted to look at Tony. The gaze she gave him over her sunglasses suggested breezy confidence and amusement.

"Hello, Handsome," she trilled at him. "I've seen you talking with all the guests and was beginning to feel a little left out."

Tony had considered his efforts to get information out of the other guests and staff subtle, and was left a little dumbfounded by her odd mix of forward and flirtatious.

"I'm Magnolia," she said, extending one hand just a little.

Tony reached forward to shake it obediently, finding unexpected strength in her thick fingers. Her nails, he noted, were perfectly manicured, and she was wearing several sparkling rings.

"I'm looking for someone who knew Angelica Grayman, a guest here about three months ago who went missing. I understand you've been here that long?" Tony wondered if he sounded to her as much as if they were on opposite sides of an interview table as he did to himself.

"Honey, I've been here for more than a year," Magnolia said expansively. "I thought I was coming for a short vacation, but Shifting Sands will get under your skin like sand in your shoes if you let it."

Tony refrained from arguing against the appeal, but found himself feeling hopeful that possibly he had finally met someone who could help him find answers. The staff had been close-lipped across the board, and the owner was the worst of them. The other guests were largely short-term: happy to gossip but not useful.

"Did you know Angelica?"

"She was a shy thing," Magnolia confirmed. "Kept to herself, took meals early. She was a gorgeous Borneo bay cat, if I recall. Kind, but a little distant. I remember the search when she went missing, everyone was very concerned, but no body was ever found. Was she in some kind of trouble?"

Tony wished he knew, but gave the same brush-off that he answered other curiosity with: "I'm just trying to find out if she might have gone somewhere from here. Did she ever mention another possible destination after Shifting Sands?"

Magnolia rolled one shoulder in a shrug. "Not to me, she didn't. Sorry I can't be of more help, *cher*."

Tony believed her. "Thank you anyway," he said gruffly.

Magnolia smiled at him, and he realized that she was one of the most unsettlingly beautiful people that he'd ever met, every inch of her generous flesh glowing with self-confidence and sincerity. He felt somehow *better* after talking with her, even so briefly.

He looked up to see Jimmy, one of the handymen who worked for Scarlet, coming out of the pool mechanical and laundry rooms. Any peaceful feeling that Magnolia had left him with vanished into irritation at the thought of Scarlet.

He got up abruptly, muttered a polite farewell, and walked past the pool to head for his cottage. It was time to stop pussy-footing around and get some answers from Scarlet.

But first, he'd put on clothes.

Chapter 3

THE RESORT WAS LAID out in a crescent, with tiers of cottages along one side. There were grassy lawns and tidy white gravel footpaths throughout, with beautifully groomed bushes providing privacy for each of the cottages. The large dining hall and recreation buildings were in the center of the layout, with a hotel building and several private-looking residences on the other side overlooking cliffs.

All Amber could see of them from here were the gleaming tile roofs. Beyond those, she could see the glint of the pool area, the beach just past it, and then the incredible stretch of blue ocean. She could just hear the pound of the distant surf over the sound of the wind ruffling the tropical plant leaves.

As she walked along the winding path towards her own personal mark on the map, she marveled at the beautiful landscaping—it was all the perfect blend of tame and wild, and she was so busy admiring the array of flowers that she nearly walked into a gardener who was trimming back some wild brush.

He was wearing a long-sleeved shirt with the resort logo and full-length pants, but neither did much to hide the fact that he was incredibly ripped beneath them; arms as thick as her legs were wielding huge cutters as if they weighed nothing.

"Sorry," Amber said breathlessly, juggling her carry-ons. It was a shame that the staff didn't partake in the clothing optional portion of the resort, she thought with a sudden streak of mischief.

The gardener did nothing but glare at her accusingly, as if she had deliberately interrupted a personal moment. Finally, he grunted a grudging apology and moved his wheelbarrow out of her way.

Amber had to rip her eyes away and walk forward. She smiled to herself as she went. Maybe she could indulge a little vacation fantasy of hers while she was here and find a hot shifter for a roll in the sheets. One-night stands weren't her sort of thing, but on vacation, one didn't have to act entirely in character.

Amber giggled to herself, remembering Scarlet's rule against predation. Did men count?

She glanced back at the gardener, who was chopping down branches angrily. Someone a little friendlier would be nice.

The path wandered past several cottages that were far, far too grand for Amber's mental picture of a cottage. Amber had booked one of the budget options that the resort offered, and even that felt like a ridiculous luxury; she wondered what the prices were on these larger cousins, with their sprawling floorplans, stained-glass windows, and shrouded private porches.

Her own cottage was the perfect size—a charming little fairy-tale house with a vine-covered entrance and a little outdoor shower. She entered with a flutter of anticipation.

The front room had a comfortable bent-wicker couch and matching chairs, upholstered in tropical florals, and an antique-looking writing desk with an anachronistically modern office chair. A steamer chest acted as the coffee table, and there were brightly painted wooden masks along most of the walls.

The downhill side of the room was a row of glass siding doors with screens that opened onto a narrow covered porch. A table and two chairs were off to one side on the deck, where she could just see down to the ocean through the jungle trees.

Amber stepped into the bedroom and gave the king-sized bed an experimental bounce. It was an exceptionally good mattress and a tall dresser with a matching vanity promised room for an entire closet of clothing. Amber dumped the contents of her carry-ons into two of the drawers, where they looked tiny and insignificant and untidy.

Amber thought about heading down to the beach or the dining hall, but the peace and quiet let all of her travel exhaustion catch up with her. After the endless drone of the flight from San Jose, and the bumpy road with Jimmy-who-wouldn't-shut-up, it was so lovely to be alone and still for a while.

She thought about how warm and muggy it was, about purring contentedly, and then she was stepping out of loose clothing in her mountain cat form and leaping up onto the big bed for a delicious nap.

Chapter 4

THE RESORT MANAGER, Scarlet, was not in her office when Tony got there.

Jimmy, the sharp-faced man who apparently did all manner of odd jobs, was hauling an impressive collection of matched luggage out of the resort van.

"Scarlet is probably down at the pool lounge," Jimmy said with a shrug. "We lost our bartender last week, and she's had to stand in."

"Lost your bartender?" Tony asked—too intensely, he realized belatedly.

"Moved back to Minnesota to take care of a sick mother or something," Jimmy said, dropping a gigantic suitcase on its side and wrestled it back upright.

Tony used a foot to stop the suitcase from rolling down the slight incline, and let Jimmy grab its handle.

"I could use a drink," he tried to say casually. He was supposed to be just another rich shifter on vacation, he reminded himself.

"You and me both," Jimmy said jovially. "That's my first stop after I deliver these. There's this hot new cat shifter that's just arrived, and I'm hoping she'll be the *social* type."

Tony had no interest in chasing tail, no matter how literal that phrase was here, and left Jimmy with a grunt to stomp down the trail to the bar at the pool. By this point, the sun had set over the ocean, and twilight was making a brief stay before full night took hold.

Scarlet was indeed at the bar, pouring and delivering drinks for a few tables of groups and couples who were laughing together.

"What can I get you?" she asked stiffly, with a scowl that Tony recognized from the mirror. She was no more suited to the social aspects of bartending than Tony was to relaxing on vacation.

Voice down, with a glance at the nearest table of revelers, Tony suggested, "You can get me the information I requested days ago. I'm sure you've had time to check my credentials by now."

Tony had not suspected that Scarlet's face could get colder, but it did.

"I haven't had time to spit in a pot," she said sharply. "If you haven't noticed, I'm a little shorthanded right now."

"I *need* that information," Tony growled at her.

"And I need to protect my guests' privacy," Scarlet answered just as fiercely. "You'll get your answers when I have *proper* assurance that you are who you say you are."

Keeping his temper had never been a strong point, and everything about Scarlet rubbed Tony wrong. "I've been very nice about asking," he said through bared teeth. "I could get the records myself."

Scarlet did not appear to be in the slightest bit intimidated. "I doubt you could," she said scathingly. Tony couldn't decide from her tone if she was dubious about his ability to force her to turn them over, or his ability to manage the most basic of alphabetic filing systems.

Tony might have answered more heatedly, but Magnolia's voice from a far table called, "Scarlet, darling! Another margarita for me!"

Scarlet waved back, and asked Tony through gritted teeth. "Can I get you a *drink*? Or would you like to continue monopolizing my time for something I won't give you?"

"A beer," Tony conceded. "And a shot of whiskey."

If he wasn't going to be able to conduct any business, there was no point in acting business-like. Besides, it kept up his cover of being on vacation.

He turned on his stool and let her get to work behind the bar while he analyzed the other occupants of the bar. Magnolia sat with a trio of well-dressed men and they were laughing together like old friends. The next table looked like an escaped troupe of actors from the set of a bad Hollywood western, complete with cigars and cowboy hats. They were playing cards, very enthusiastically.

A boy who looked too young to even be in the bar was hitting on a table of middle-aged women wearing terrible jewelry who were giggling at him indulgently. An elderly couple was sitting further out onto the deck, looking out over the pool and nursing glasses of wine.

Jimmy had apparently delivered the recalcitrant luggage, and was lingering near the self-serve snacks that were opposite the back entrance to the bar.

"Your drinks," Scarlet said, putting them in front of him with a little more force than necessary before swishing off to take orders from the table of card players.

Tony turned to take the shot of whiskey just as a new figure appeared in the doorway and paused to look around.

She was petite and curvy, with a curtain of black hair and medium-toned skin. She wore simple khaki shorts and a collared shirt, and she filled them up absolutely perfectly. The shirt was unbuttoned a tantalizing way, showing more than a hint of the curves of her breasts. Somehow, that was even sexier than the fully nude women who pranced around the resort in their heels. Her short, straight nose was the center of a round face, and her big, thickly-lashed eyes looked golden from this distance.

Pretty girls didn't usually turn Tony's head, and he certainly hadn't come to Shifting Sands looking for companionship, but something about the figure woke his tiger. If he had been in that form, his ears would be perked in her direction.

He realized he was staring just as her gaze swept the room and caught his. He downed the shot of whiskey in a moment of wild confusion and the next several seconds were a heated haze of pain as the fiery shifter-strength liquid went down the wrong pipe and he had to cough himself back to breathing. When his eyes had stopped watering enough to look around again, the gorgeous woman was right next to him, smiling invitingly. "Buy you a drink?" she offered.

"You do know that this is an all-inclusive resort?" Tony had to ask, looking around as if to make sure that it was, because between the burning whiskey and her proximity, nothing made sense.

*That's **her***, his tiger and all of his instincts were telling him, but after years of waiting to meet his one mate, Tony couldn't believe either his amazing luck or his awful sense of timing.

It didn't matter that he was at the resort on business, and potentially unfortunate business at that. It didn't matter that he hadn't given much thought to settling down. One look at this woman's light brown eyes, and he was hopelessly, entirely lost in her.

All of his vague ideas about what a mate meant went straight out the window. This wasn't about lust, or at least, not only lust. He knew this woman to bottom of his soul, and she was everything he'd ever wanted in another person, all wrapped up in what was easily the sexiest package he'd ever seen.

Chapter 5

AMBER LINGERED OUTSIDE the entrance to the pool bar, agonizing over how many buttons to leave open on her shirt, and finally went in.

She had just decided she liked how much cleavage was showing when she caught sight of Jimmy, that odious chatterbox from the resort van, and it was everything she could do not to button her shirt up to her chin. A quick assessment of the room showed that everyone else there was with someone, except for a big, broad-shouldered man who was leaning on the bar itself.

Perfect!

He turned away from her approach to take a shot of alcohol from the counter, then coughed and sputtered ungracefully as Amber shimmied herself over to his elbow with the transparent excuse of getting a drink from the bar.

"Can I buy you a drink?" she blurted, hoping she looked sexy and not just desperate.

The man was even dreamier up close. He had beautifully-muscled arms, and a square jaw straight out of a superhero comic. He had brown eyes and dark brown hair, barely long enough to show some wave, and a smoldering look that unsettled Amber to her toes. It was like he had been lifted, word for word, out of her teenage dream diary.

She had never had such an immediate, physical attraction to someone and she felt oddly as if he was meant entirely for her.

But that was idiotic.

Much like she was.

"You do know that this is an all-inclusive resort?" he asked her, glancing around.

He was probably looking for an escape route.

Amber felt her face heat, and blessed her unknown progenitors for giving her skin that would mostly hide her blush. "Oh, ah, yes," she stammered, then chose honesty as her best path from there. "I'm sorry, I just didn't want to get caught alone with *him*."

She tried to subtly raise her eyebrows in Jimmy's direction, and probably only looked like she was having some kind of seizure.

"Who, Jimmy?" He looked around to the far side of the bar, and made no effort to keep his voice down. Fortunately, a rowdy group of shifters playing cards had a timely moment of noisy celebration and woe.

Failing to actually sink into her barstool and die, Amber said between clenched teeth, "Very subtle. Do you work undercover often?"

That made him nearly fall off his own barstool with a start. "I beg your pardon?"

Surprised by his reaction, Amber put up innocent hands. "It's just... that wasn't very slick. Okay, you know what, let's try this again." She put out a hand. "I'm Amber. I'll just order a drink and go if you'd like."

"Tony," he said, taking her hand and clinging to it like a drowning man. "Please don't go."

Gratified and surprised by his reaction, Amber gave his hand a shake that was a little more lingering than polite. "Okay," she said with a little laugh.

Scarlet had the beautiful timing to return from handing out drinks and ask brusquely, "What can I get you?"

"Something fruity," Amber said. "With an umbrella. I'm not picky."

She caught a glimpse of Jimmy out of the corner of one eye trying to catch her gaze and made a point of pretending not to see him. It wasn't a hardship to gaze at Tony as if he had all of her attention. He was probably the most masculine thing that Amber had ever had an excuse to talk to, all rippling muscles and jaw, and he had an amazingly expressive mouth.

Scarlet frowned and went to the other end of the bar to make her drink.

"Have you been here long?" Amber asked. "At the resort, I mean? Not the bar. Of course."

"A *week*," Tony said.

The way he said it made it sound like a finals week, or a week of torture, not a vacation at an upscale beach resort with all the gourmet food and fine alcohol you could want.

"I've got a week here, too," Amber volunteered. "It would have been nice to stay longer, especially after such a long plane ride to get here, but it's hard to get time off of work."

"Oh? Where do you work?" Tony asked.

"Just a little local garden store in Lakefield," Amber said with a shrug. "But I'm the only employee other than the owner and his wife, and they lean on me to do a lot of the day-to-day work."

"I don't have a green thumb," Tony said, as if it were a great confession. "I killed a jade plant once."

"They're surprisingly easy to over-water if you don't give them good drainage," Amber said understandingly. "How about you? Where do you work?"

"I work for an... er... in construction. *Management*. In, uh, construction."

Amber wondered where he really worked, but didn't press the issue. If he wanted to elevate himself to management to impress someone at a resort bar, she could understand why. After all, she was the one wearing her shirt one more button open than usual, and she was loving the way his eyes couldn't entirely keep from straying from her face as they spoke. Did that make her a floozy?

The idea alarmed her until she reminded herself that she was on vacation, and had come determined to live outside of her comfortable little box of wholesomeness for the week. She would probably never see this guy again. That idea gave her an unexpected pang of bone-deep regret, which she squashed as quickly as she could. Her cat gave an unexpected growl of disagreement.

This one is ours, her cat said, but didn't explain the cryptic idea.

Scarlet arrived with a brilliantly colored drink sporting not only an umbrella, but several pieces of fruit on a plastic cocktail sword. Amber gave a delighted "Ooo!" as she picked it up, but Scarlet didn't linger to appreciate her reaction.

"I wonder what her animal is," Amber said wryly, taking a long sip of her technicolor drink. It definitely met her requirements for being fruity, and it had a delightful kick that promised plenty of alcohol and went straight to her head. "It's funny that she knows that about every one of us, and we don't know a thing about her."

"She's probably a wolverine," Tony ground out between clenched teeth. Scarlet clearly failed to amuse him.

Were they lovers at odds? Amber caught herself wondering. There was certainly some kind of *tension* shimmering between them. She took another long drink. "What about you?"

Tony looked like she'd caught him in headlights. "What about me?"

"Your, er... animal?"

"Tiger!" he said, as if relieved. "Siberian tiger, to be exact." And as an afterthought, "You?"

"Cat," Amber said cautiously, and the heady drink made her continue when otherwise she might not have. "An Andean mountain cat, actually."

Tony's eyebrows raised. "I've never even heard of that."

Everyone said that.

"It's like a snow leopard," Amber explained. "But smaller, the size of a big housecat."

"It sounds pretty." The way he said it, gazing straight at her, made Amber warm to her toes and her cat purred in her ears.

She took another sip of her drink and, between the slight buzz of alcohol and the delight in Tony's attentive company, felt deliciously not herself at all.

The moment was doused by an unwelcome intrusion. "Are you finding your way around all right, Amber?"

Jimmy sidled up to her far side, and Amber felt obliged to turn politely, after casting a desperate look at Tony. "Ah, yes. Everything is quite well marked."

Her neutral tone was meant to be discouraging, but Jimmy sat on the stool beside her in chummy oblivion.

"You be sure to let me know if you need anything, then. I could arrange a fishing trip in the boat, if you're interested. Or a tour of the arboretum at Mr. Big's estate..."

Amber knew immediately that she hadn't hidden her transparent interest in the last quickly enough, and took another desperate slurp at the bottom of her drink with a non-committal noise before she could ask any encouraging questions about what kind of plants Mr. Big grew.

"We were just leaving," Tony said unexpectedly from her other side.

Amber looked at him in surprise and not a little delight. He sounded... jealous. Protective. It helped that when he stood up, he towered over them, and Jimmy actually shrunk back a little in instinctive alarm.

She gladly played along, pushing back her empty glass, then impulsively grabbing the drink umbrella as she stood up. "Thanks," she said, officially at Jimmy, but more meaningfully at Tony.

If Tony rushed her towards to the back door a little with his long legs, she scampered nothing less than eagerly with him.

Chapter 6

THE AIR OUTSIDE THE bar felt cooler and fresher, and it was abruptly quiet as the door closed behind them. The colorful lights of the bar gave way to a thickly-scented, dark path, barely made navigable by a series of lights.

Tony felt the angry prickle that Jimmy had inspired immediately soothe as they paused to let their eyes adjust.

"I'm sorry," he said at once, looking down at the top of Amber's head. Her hair was sleek and touchable, and it was everything he could do not to stroke her in a too-familiar way. "I shouldn't have presumed to tell Jimmy that we were leaving. If you wanted another drink, or to stay at the bar..."

Amber tilted her head to look up at him, her eyes bright in the darkness. "You were my white knight," she said, with no hint of sarcasm. "That man will not take a hint. Seriously, maybe his animal is a *leech*."

"I'd put money on a rodent," Tony said, smiling.

For an oddly long moment, they stood and just stared at each other. Tony suspected that neither of them was thinking about Jimmy.

His *mate*. He couldn't believe how gorgeous and curvy she was, or how comfortable he felt, just being near her. He wanted her more than he had ever wanted anything in his memory.

When he bent to kiss her, unable to resist, she didn't even hesitate, but flung eager arms around his neck and kissed him back, standing on tiptoe to reach him. She tasted like alcohol and fruit, and her mouth managed to be both pliable and firm.

"My cottage," he offered, between kisses. He barely had the self-control not to wrestle her willingly into the fragrant tropical bushes.

"Mmm, yes!" she said, but she didn't stop kissing him, or raking fingers through his hair.

Even with her agreement, Tony found that he couldn't stop touching her or move his feet. Finally, he picked her up, and she gave a squeal of delighted laughter and wrapped her legs around his waist.

He could move then, though he recognized that he was staggering and weaving in his path. She didn't hamper him with weight, but the way she squirmed against him with her mostly bare legs drove him absolutely mad and her kisses left him dizzy. He had never realized how much having someone touch his shoulders could turn him on.

"Wait, wait!" Amber laughed against his lips, just as they turned on the path to his cottage.

"What? What is it?" His voice sounded like begging to his own ears.

"I lost my sandal!"

He put her down, carefully, sliding her down over the erection that was bulging his shorts, hands lingering at her waist.

She gave a gratifying moan of desire as her feet touched the ground, and she stood there leaning into him for a moment longer than was necessary.

"Your sandal?" Tony prompted.

"Screw the sandal," Amber said fiercely, and then they were tangled in kisses again as Tony tried to remember where he'd put his cottage key.

Between digging it out and trying to claim Amber's mouth for his own, Tony managed to maneuver them into the entrance of the house and finesse the door open—which is how it stayed as they began the erotic struggle of removing each article of clothing and finding the bedroom.

"Crap," he said suddenly, when he'd gotten her shirt off and she had thrown his across the room.

"It's not that complicated a bra," Amber promised, big golden eyes laughing. "I can help you."

"No, it's... condoms. I didn't bring condoms."

That gave her pause, but it was a grateful pause, and the smile that bloomed across her face was more reward than he had expected. "You really are a white knight," she said warmly. "I'm on the pill, if it makes you feel better."

The pause changed the timbre of the urgency, but not the magnitude. Tony wanted her more badly than ever, and gathered her into his arms for a deep kiss. He cradled both sides of her face, her silky hair spilling over his hands, and let his tongue explore the depths of her mouth.

She slid her arms around his neck and kissed back, licking and twining his tongue until they were both panting for breath.

He laid her down on the big bed and kissed down her neck, loving the way her body arched to his fingers. He stroked her bare arms, and over her bra, down her sides, and she closed her eyes and purred at him in delight. He put fingers along the waistband of her shorts, but when she raised her hips in invitation to remove them, only stroked her side again, and kissed between her breasts while she squirmed.

It was his first time with his mate, and he wanted to savor it as long as he could.

Amber had other plans, and gave a little frustrated growl when he ignored her signals. She pushed him off with more strength than he expected from her short frame, and he rolled over onto his back on the bed willingly while she straddled him. Her loose hair brushed his chest as she put an arm on either side of him and leaned down to kiss and nibble at his chest. Then she sat up again, and deftly unfastened her own bra, letting it spill off of her and release the breasts he had been vainly trying not to stare at all evening.

They were perfect orbs of firm flesh, with big nipples that were hard with desire, and he could no more keep his hands from them than deny that this woman was his one perfect, fated companion.

She moaned as he cupped them, threw back her head in ecstasy, and ground herself against the thick erection that was only a few light layers of clothing away. Tony wasn't sure what he would have done without those layers; he was at such a fever pitch that he would have embarrassed himself like a first-time teenager without the cloth to dull the sensation a little.

He used his thumbs to make lazy circles around her areolas, then dragged them across the erect nipples, and she gave a little cry of pleasure that made him feel proud and powerful. He did it again, with a little squeeze of his hands of the beautiful, soft flesh of her breasts. She cried out again in appreciation, scratching him reflexively, then tipped her head down to look at him and beg, "I want you..."

The shorts were no longer welcome in the bed, and there was an acrobatic flurry as they both tried frantically to shed them, without withdrawing from each other more than absolutely necessarily. The moment they were fully naked, he had to hold her against him, just enjoying the silky length of her warm body beside his, and then he was slipping into her wet, soft folds without a hint of resistance.

He gave her a slow, careful thrust, burying himself into her in one smooth, careful motion, fighting himself for control. To his shock, she arched in his arms, crying out in intense pleasure and shuddering in unexpected orgasm. He had to bite his lip to keep from taking her with abandon then, but gave a second slow, contained thrust, trying to keep her at that plateau of pleasure.

Her next cry was less, but still powerful, and she opened astonished eyes to meet his gaze as he rolled her onto her back without unlocking from her. His third thrust was less controlled, and she lifted her hips to eagerly meet him as her fingers raked across his shoulders.

It was like swimming in a hot pool of pleasure, thrusting into her. She was a heady mix of pliable and resistant, and the bite of her fingernails on his arms as she held him and moaned was an intoxicating aphrodisiac. Tony realized he was growling with need and kissed her, nibbling at her ear as gently as he could manage.

He had to stop doing that, his entire world narrowing to concentrating on putting off his own mounting release until he realized that Amber was crying out in orgasmic pleasure again; the sound of her delight was too much for him to resist and he was filling her with his hot seed.

His frantic thrusts slowed at last, and he was gradually aware again of the room around them, the chirps of insects and frogs outside, and the door of the cottage, still wide open.

Chapter 7

AMBER CAME BACK TO herself slowly as Tony's thrusts tapered off into a finishing rhythm. They continued to couple in the afterglow of the pleasure, as long as possible, and finally lay next to each other in gleeful exhaustion as their panting breath returned to normal.

When she had decided to treat the vacation as an excuse to cut loose, she had not expected it to feel anywhere near this... natural. She felt more comfortable with this complete stranger than she had ever been with anyone she had ever known, and he had taken her to heights she'd never dreamed existed. She hadn't even known it was possible to orgasm at a first thrust; this man was clearly no stranger to giving a woman pleasure.

His hand, still making lazy circles on her belly and breasts, promised more, if she was brave enough to accept it.

It's just a vacation fling, she reminded herself, and she thrust away the pang of regret that came with the practicality. Nothing about their encounter suggested he was any more interested in a relationship that extended past the boundaries of the resort than she was, and she ought to be grateful for that.

Her plan had always been to go home to Minnesota after a week of freedom, pick the least objectionable of the shy farmboys who made eyes at her at the garden supply store and start a perfectly respectable family. She couldn't let a magnetic tiger shifter tempt her away from that practical path, no matter how intensely her inner mountain cat was trying to convince her that this was something *more*, something *better*.

This week, she would take each day as it came and fixedly *not* think about what would come afterwards.

It was hard, though, to watch Tony get up and bring them towels to clean up with, and not think about how he made every one of those farmboys look spindly, pale, and utterly unappealing in comparison.

"I, ah... that was... thank you! Wow!" Amber said, not sure what else to say but aware that something was in order.

Tony smiled at her, a beautiful, confident smile that warmed Amber to her toes, and leaned over to kiss her possessively. "I was just thinking the exact same thing."

"I should get my sandal," she giggled against his lips after a lengthy kiss. "And close the front door..."

His cottage came with bathrobes, and she gratefully slipped into one and padded outside with a flashlight as Tony picked up their clothing and tidied the bed.

She leaned against the doorframe with her rescued sandal on one finger, watching as he deftly shook the comforter back into shape. It was refreshing, watching such a big, manly-looking male make a bed. His long arms served him well; he was able to fluff it with one smooth motion, where Amber would have been running from corner to corner.

He shot her a sideways smile that indicated that he knew she was watching him. "Seven sisters," he said. "Every one of them was a tomboy and I got all the housekeeping chores they could stick me with."

"That's adorable," Amber said wistfully. She shut the door behind her as she came into the room.

"You're an only child?" Tony guessed, and it was close to the heart.

"I... don't know," Amber admitted guardedly. "I was left on the front porch of a church, and I don't know if I actually had *any* siblings."

She expected pity. That was the usual reaction when she confessed the details of her childhood, and she already regretted bringing it up.

This was supposed to be a no-strings holiday fling, with no place for intimate discussions. They should be talking about fishing, or the weather, or the next time he was planning to tumble her into bed. Which was not nearly soon enough, as far as Amber was concerned. She had never felt such an odd combination of sated and needy.

"There's a shower," Tony suggested, gesturing towards the bathroom door. He winked and added, "It's big enough for two."

Amber let the bathrobe slide the floor behind her as she sauntered in the direction he had indicated. "That's good," she purred. "Because I may not leave you any hot water, otherwise..."

Tony scrambled to follow her.

The bathroom was tiled in blue, with windows out over dark foliage outside. Amber had to stand on tiptoe to see out of them, but Tony would have no trouble enjoying the view... if he had eyes for anything but Amber. She loved the way he watched her, and left the glass door open while she slipped in and turned on the water.

His cottage was fancier than her own, and where she had only a narrow, simple shower, his was, as promised, plenty big enough for two, with a tiled bench along one side that she was already making plans for. His bathroom also had a Jacuzzi tub, opposite the shower, and Tony sat down on the edge of it with a wide grin, watching.

Once the water was warm, Amber soaped herself to a tantalizing lather, keenly aware of his gaze, and playfully dressed herself in bubbles. A glance showed that he was enjoying the show; his generous member was already beginning to swell again. She rinsed off the bubbles and soaped herself more earnestly, bending away from him to rub her legs and give a view of her wet ass, and then turning to pay exaggerated attention to each breast under the warm stream of water.

Tony had to adjust his seat on the edge of the tub, but remained an audience, rather than a participant. Amber felt like this was an unspoken challenge, and let her hands trail down her sides and belly, to lay one hand, fingers flat, against the mound of her entrance. She'd been uncertain about the Brazilian wax that she'd gotten before her vacation, but now it felt daring, and deliciously exposed. She let her fingers trail over each nearby thigh, and reveled in the smooth, velvety texture.

She peeked up to see if Tony was still attending to her and was pleased to see that he was at *full* attention. He had one leg stretched up on the ledge of the tub and his gorgeous member was erect again, as if it were reaching for her. Tony had both hands behind him, as if it was all he could do to keep his hands from himself, and Amber suddenly wanted to see him touch it.

She wriggled her hips a little, and let a single finger dip into the folds of her entrance, hoping he would take the hint.

Though she had done it for Tony's watching pleasure, she couldn't keep back the gasp of pleasure it gave her; she was still swollen and sensitive from their earlier activity, and the touch of her own finger brought her back to a fever pitch of desire and need. She gave another tentative stroke, and another, and looked up to find that Tony's look had intensified, and the lines of his hard body were rippled with clenched muscle.

He still hadn't touched the rigid hard-on that was all Amber could focus on.

She put a second finger in, enjoying the sensation, but so aware that it was nothing compared to the thick, solid member that was so close and yet so far away. She gave one slow stroke, and then another, unable to keep from squirming at her own touch. The water pouring over her shoulders added another dimension of sensation, and she closed her eyes to tip her head back and let it pour over her face.

A groan made her open her eyes, and she found that Tony was touching himself at last, not stroking, but holding his member tightly with a closed fist, as if he could keep his pleasure from mounting too fast by sheer will.

She didn't want to stop touching herself, but she was dizzy with desire for more; she wanted to be filled by his cock, not just admire it, and the memory of his movement inside of her was an ache. "Tony..." she moaned, and speaking out loud unlocked the moment.

Amber wasn't even sure how he crossed the room, but suddenly Tony was against her, lifting her onto the bench and kissing her neck as he pressed himself against her hungry folds.

She welcomed him eagerly, taking the length of him into her in a single, deep thrust that seemed to split her, fill her, and complete her, all at once. She didn't come at his first entrance this time, but did again after only a few of his strong penetrations, cresting into pleasure with a helpless cry.

He slowed, carefully, and then picked her up again and turned so that the water was spilling down over her back and she was straddling him as he sat back against the bench. She rode him, letting her fingernails trail over his shoulders and arms, reveling in the devoted attention he gave her breasts and the small of her back. He held her close, like she was a precious thing, while he met each of her bounces with a wild thrust of his own, and his embrace became a desperate clutch as he lost himself inside her once more.

Chapter 8

THE PRACTICAL SIDE of Tony was dimly grateful that they were already in a shower and it was easy to clean up, but the rest of him knew he would never be able to take another shower without picturing Amber, her own fingers caressing herself, her gorgeous hair flowing wet over her bare shoulders, lips parted in concentration and desire.

He soaped Amber gently, and let her do the same with him. They explored each other's bodies curiously, fingers stroking over flesh like they were taking silent notes. She lingered over the angry scars on his back, but didn't ask. He stroked the faint scars on her wrist, but didn't ask.

It still felt unreal, finding her. He'd known his mate was out there, somewhere, but it was a distant certainty, playing no role in his real life. To find her, to so completely trust and love her so quickly, gave the whole world a new cast, as if the sun had suddenly changed color.

And the sex!

Tony grinned, looking down at her hair as she finger-combed the conditioner through it. What a wildcat!

They toweled each other off with the same gentle silence, and without conferring, each took a side of the big king bed and snuggled in together.

In the darkness, cuddled together, Tony felt like he could ask, "Was it hard, growing up without siblings? There were days I'd wish for it, when privacy was impossible to get in our little house..."

Amber was quiet for a moment, and Tony wondered if he'd pushed too far, too fast.

Then she said, "It was a small town, and they really did their best for me. The staff at the church where I was found, Saint Mary's, they still call me their little foundling and send me birthday cards every year on the anniversary of when I was found. And foster care was... it really wasn't horrible or abusive, like you read about in the news sometimes. But I was a difficult child even before I started turning into a cat when I got mad. I went through a few families before I aged out."

Tony held her tighter, nuzzling her neck in wordless comfort.

After a few breaths, she continued. "I finally found someone like me in high school—a bear shifter named Alice who told me there were others like us. We stayed in touch, even after she moved away, and we ended up sharing an apartment back in Lakefield after college. She's the one who convinced me to come here. I was... I was hoping I'd find another Andean mountain cat, like me. Maybe figure out where I came from, why I was abandoned."

The hopelessness in her voice would have cut Tony to the bone even if he hadn't already loved her. "You don't have to be alone anymore," he said fiercely. "You can make your own family."

Amber went rigid in his arms and Tony had a stab of doubt. Was it possible that she didn't consider him her mate, or that she didn't want him for family despite their connection? The idea that she might not feel their bond as deeply as he did made him suddenly, deeply uneasy.

They lay stiffly together, a chorus of frogs and insects loud compared to their silence, until Amber gradually relaxed in his arms. It took Tony a long while to realize that she had fallen asleep, and it took him even longer to fall asleep himself.

HE WOKE UP TANGLED in Amber, arms and legs entwined with hers. He'd never slept over with a girlfriend, always preferring to seek his own space, and he was amazed by how familiar it felt to come awake next to another person. It was fascinating to feel her breathing change against his chest, to feel her stir along the whole length of him, and come awake in parts; her toes wiggled adorably before the rest of her woke.

"Good morning," he said in her ear.

There was enough late morning light streaming in through the window to see her clearly. She looked confused at first, then wary, then smiled slowly.

"Good morning," she replied, almost shyly.

He bent over to kiss her, and she responded hungrily, wrapping her arms around his neck and holding him close to her. Any doubts that Tony had been left with from the night before were washed away in the wave of passion and the complete rightness that came from being so close to her. She could have no doubts about *his* interest; his member was rigid between them, and she was rubbing herself against it wantonly.

"We'll miss breakfast," she teased, drawing away from his kisses.

"I know what I want for breakfast," he growled back at her.

He slid fingers down into her and found that she was as ready for him as he was for her, wet and slick and warm. He touched her for a long moment, loving the way her breath caught and her body tensed.

"Oh, please, please," she finally begged, when Tony had teased her to a fine sweat.

He rolled over to straddle and take her, slipping, unresisted, into her folds as she moaned and gave a sweet cry of delight.

If waking to his mate in his arms had felt like delicious rightness, waking to take his mate so intimately seemed like heavenly choruses and perfection. He groaned in need and pleasure, keeping his strokes careful and tender.

She squirmed in blissful torture as he rode her, and cried out in abandon as he brought her to the crests of pleasure, not once, but twice, before he could no longer keep his own release in check, thrusting in increasing need and wildness until he was spent.

"I'm *sore*," Amber said, but it was with undeniable satisfaction. She held him tight against her until their breathing had returned to normal.

Tony couldn't help but feel pleased by the statement, and he nibbled her ear in wordless delight.

Chapter 9

AMBER COULDN'T REMEMBER ever feeling so complete.

When she was with Tony, she forgot every insecurity she'd ever felt. He seemed like *family*, and it was easy to ignore the fact that she'd only just met him. Too easy.

She propped herself up on an elbow when he rolled out of the bed, and watched him go, mesmerized by the gorgeous curve of his ass as he went.

When he was gone, it was easier to remember that this was only a resort fling, that she was only a beach diversion, and he was only a last wild ride before she settled into something... less.

Things this perfect don't last, she reminded herself. Too many foster families as a child had taught her to mistrust things that seemed so good.

She would enjoy this—to the bottom of her soul, she would enjoy this—and then she would go home and get on with her life, however she could.

Her determination to enjoy the day carried them through a swift shower—more utilitarian than the one the night before—to the dining hall for breakfast, where they found that service in the restaurant was already over. There was still an extensive buffet, with a range of breakfast and lunch choices (just being put out), fresh fruit, crusty bread, and an array of salty snacks and vegetables.

They piled plates high, and went out to a set of seats overlooking the pool.

"Are you eating raw broccoli? Ew!" Tony had taken a plate heavy on meat and bread, while Amber had been enraptured by the fresh options of vegetables and exotic fruits. They both had been unable to resist the rolls that had been brought fresh from the oven while they were serving themselves.

"You don't like broccoli?" Amber dipped a piece into a puddle of creamy dressing and ate it with relish.

"Not raw," Tony said, shaking his head emphatically. "And not unless it's smothered in cheese."

"I didn't like fresh vegetables until I started growing them myself," Amber confessed. "There's something about the taste of things you've put your own sweat and tears into." She had to admit that the selection here was better than anything she could grow, and she wondered if the resort had its own garden or greenhouse.

They compared favorite foods—agreeing on cheeses and breads, but disagreeing about meats.

"I like a meat you have to fight with," Tony said with a sparkling grin.

"I prefer mine fully cooked and not recognizable," Amber countered. "Give me a casserole or a sausage any day."

"You're from the Midwest," Tony said sagely.

They made short work of their plates and went back for a second round of fresh-ground coffee—Amber could not resist snagging a sweet roll on her way back to their table, and Tony took a second plate of food nearly as large as the first.

Amber enjoyed the warmth of the sun on her skin as she lingered over the combination of flavors in her mouth. She also enjoyed watching Tony eat, more than she'd ever thought she would take pleasure in such a mundane task. His fingers were so sure, and his jaw as he chewed was so obviously strong. He was wearing a short-sleeved, collared shirt that shrouded most of his shoulders, but the strength of them was still obvious, and his arms were thick and tanned. It was like watching a work of art, or a dance performance.

"What are your plans for the day?" Amber asked, when she realized she was staring at him again.

Tony looked reflexively at his wrist, though there was no watch there, or even a tan-line indicating he'd even worn one since he'd arrived. He scowled at the spot as if it reminded him of something.

"I hadn't made any plans." Then he grinned. "I wouldn't mind any day that ended like yesterday did."

Amber blushed, and was glad all over again that her skin wouldn't show it easily. She loved the way he looked at her, like she was delicious and desirable and perfect.

"I was thinking about swimming," she said with a nod to the pool to cover her confusion. "It's a lovely pool, and it might be too hot to enjoy in the afternoon."

Already, the temperature was baking hot, the sun beating down on the tile. Summer at Lakefield could get muggy and hot, but there was an intensity to the sun here that she wasn't used to.

She looked at Tony. There were a lot of intensities here she wasn't used to. "And then I was looking at maybe getting a massage or a pedicure, or something ridiculously girly like that."

Tony did his best to look innocent as he asked, "Are you planning to take advantage of the resort's skinny-dipping-encouraged policy?"

Amber flushed again. "I'm not that brave," she said with a laugh. "I brought a bikini that I barely have the guts to wear."

"I can't wait to see it," Tony said sincerely. He had the grace to not look disappointed that Amber wasn't going to be lounging nude on the pool deck and actually seemed eager to see the promised garment. "May I join you?"

"Of course," Amber said with a slow smile.

To her surprise, Tony took her invitation to mean the entire day. He scheduled his own tandem massage and pedicure with the manager of the spa when Amber did, before she retreated for her own cottage to procure the promised bikini.

"I don't plan on getting any toe polish," he said with a wink. "But I do need a nail trim, and who doesn't like a little pampering?"

The idea of a big, manly man like Tony putting up with pampering gave Amber a skip to her step as she returned to the pool, too wrapped up in her thoughts of him to feel self-conscious in her admittedly skimpy swimwear. It helped that she passed a nude couple that gave friendly nods without the slightest trace of embarrassment.

With his closer cottage, he got back to the pool before she did, and she paused to observe him for a long moment in the shadowed entrance.

There were other guests enjoying the pool—one older man was swimming diligent laps, and a few individuals were sunning in the chairs at the other end of the pool—but Amber could only stare at Tony. He was wearing loose swim trunks, and lounging in one of the bar chairs with elegant ease and strength. His uncovered shoulders rippled with muscles that were pale in the golden sunlight. He had put on sunglasses, and looked like someone out of a movie, perfectly posed on a pearly white chair.

A spy movie, or an action-adventure, with that physique, Amber thought. *And he's **mine**.*

Her mountain cat was in avid agreement. *Ours,* she purred. *Forever.*

The thought caught her by surprise and she delayed in the shadows another moment.

He wasn't hers, not really. And this was temporary, even more temporary than most of the people who moved through her life. As badly as she longed for *family* and *permanent*, she was not going to find that in a wild, tropical holiday affair. She didn't even know who he *really* was.

Chapter 10

TONY CAUGHT SIGHT OF Amber hanging back under the roof of the bar, just out of the sun. Her brilliant blue bikini wasn't nearly as skimpy as he'd been led to believe, and she looked like a goddess. He couldn't help but stare. The curve of her hip, the sexy slope of her shoulders, the sleek ponytail that curled around and was long enough to tickle the mound of her breast... it was a package that he wasn't sure he'd have been able to resist even if she wasn't his mate.

She took a deep breath and started walking towards him, padding as gracefully as a cat. Tony was mesmerized by the way she moved.

When she stopped at his chair, he had to catch his breath and keep himself from reaching up and pulling her onto his lap for a kiss with no care for the other guests on the pool deck. He was going to need a dip in the unheated pool, for sure.

Amber smiled at him, a slow, tentative smile that crinkled the corners of her eyes. "Ready for a swim?"

"You have no idea," Tony replied, glad that his swimsuit had a generous cut.

The pool was long and deep enough for laps in both directions. The far end, overlooking the beach, ended in a broad set of steps that went out of the water to a wide lower deck with umbrellas and chairs. Palm trees were spaced along both long sides, and the near end had narrower steps between twin waterfalls that fell from the deck nearest the bar and the buffet. A tinny radio was playing American rock, with commercials in Spanish. They walked down these steps holding hands, and Amber gave a little gasp at the chill of the water.

"Ooooo, I'm not sure this was a good idea," Amber exclaimed, shivering closer to him and laughing.

"It'll feel good once you're in," Tony promised, but he gave his own involuntary noise of alarm as his own package hit the cold water.

Amber balked as the water hit her belly. "A chair in the sun is looking really nice right now," she said reluctantly, but she was still giggling.

Tony took a chance. "You just have to get in all at once," he said. "Get the shock over with."

Amber looked up at him with big, alarmed eyes as he reached down and scooped her up. She squealed in playful dismay as he tossed her easily into the water before them before ducking himself in after her.

He was right, of course—once they were in the water, it felt no more than cool and refreshing.

Amber splashed him back, and they romped into the deeper water and then swam in leisurely fashion to the far end by the lower deck. Tony was aware of the indulgent looks a few of the guests gave them, but most of his attention was caught by his mate.

She swam easily, like a beautiful, curvy little mermaid, and when she ducked her head under the water and came out of the water beside him, he felt a rush of amazement and adoration.

They lounged at the edge of the pool, drinking in the sparkling sunlight, and Tony gathered her close to him, pausing at every step to give her a chance to protest the intimacy. He was grateful when she snuggled close to him.

"Costa Rica is as gorgeous as all the brochures promised," Amber sighed, her bare skin against his, cradled in the water of the pool. "*Pura vida* indeed."

"More gorgeous," Tony said, smiling at her.

"You aren't looking at Costa Rica," she said, smiling back.

"I know," Tony said, and he leaned in and kissed her, as he'd been longing to do since he'd first seen her at the edge of the pool. "But there's a beautiful banana tree behind you," he teased, once he finally released her mouth.

She twisted to look behind her. "That's not a banana tree," she told him. "That's just a palm tree."

"You sure it's not a coconut tree?"

"Quite sure," Amber said confidently. "See the way the leaves hang, and the shape of the trunk?"

"Mm-hm," Tony said.

"You're not looking at the tree," Amber scolded with a smile.

"Nope," Tony agreed.

This time Amber leaned up to kiss him first, and he drew her close against him, warm compared to the cool water around them. Her buoyancy gave the embrace an extra element of movement and excitement.

"We have an hour until our massage," she suggested in his ear, once he had released her lips at last.

The hint was all he needed. They scrambled from the pool, giggling like adolescents, and they barely took the time to towel off before slipping into their sandals and retreating for Tony's cottage.

This time, they managed to get the door closed behind them.

Chapter 11

THE MASSEUSES LAUGHED off their tardy appearance to their appointment with knowing winks. "We are on tropical time here," said the woman with a thick Mexican accent. "I'm Lydia, please follow Andre."

The other masseuse, a lanky blond man with big, strong hands and an Australian accent, led them to a pair of tables in a private courtyard surrounded by beautifully flowering bushes.

Amber was amused to notice that the spa was set up for grooming animals as well as people, with a wide variety of currycombs and brushes hanging along the wall.

She nearly fell asleep during her massage, lulled by the conversation that Tony carried on with the two masseuses, all in lilting Spanish that she understood no more than a word or two of.

Afterwards, as they were getting dressed, she asked him, "You speak Spanish?"

He nodded before she could regret how foolish a question it was; clearly he spoke it very well.

"I took a little in high school," she said, feeling shy about it. "And a semester of French. Do you speak any other languages?"

"Russian," Tony said cheerfully. "Also French, Swedish, and enough Japanese and Mandarin to get by."

Amber stared, then laughed, pulling her t-shirt over her head. "Oh, just enough to get by. In construction management, you know..."

Tony startled and managed to look guilty and angry at the same time.

"Oh, look!" Amber was glad to distract him by pointing out a toucan making a lazy loop above them, but she knew that Tony was living some lie with her, and it reminded her too keenly that this fantasy had no place in either of their real lives.

A phone rang then and they looked around in surprise. Tony finally said, "Wait, that's me," and dug into his pants pocket. "I'm not used to having a signal," he said sheepishly. "Sorry, have to take this while I can!"

He left the spa hastily, already answering, and Amber was alone in the pretty little courtyard as she finished dressing.

Lydia returned with a smile. "Your young man left in quite a hurry," she observed.

"He's not my young man," Amber said swiftly.

That earned her a long, thoughtful look. "He certainly *appears* to be," Lydia said gently.

"Oh, no," Amber laughed desperately. "We just met, it's just... a vacation thing." She must sound terrifically shallow, she thought miserably. "I mean, I like him, it's just not a... he's got a... a..." a life he wouldn't tell her about. She thought about the phone call he'd had to take.

"Is he married?" Lydia asked softly.

Amber stared in horror. "No!" she said. Then, miserably, "I have no idea." She laughed, nearly hysterically. "I never even *thought* of that."

Lydia shook her head. "I do not think I would believe it," she said firmly. "Not the way that he looks at you, like he has never seen anyone *before* you."

Amber wondered if it was only because she wanted to believe Lydia so much that the idea of Tony being married really did seem impossible. It didn't feel like he was hiding a wife, it felt like he was hiding a *purpose*. Like he wasn't really here for a vacation.

He is ours, her cat agreed. *No one else's, ever.*

"These things work out the way they are supposed to," the masseuse said confidently, looking into her eyes. "Let yourself enjoy this. Seize it."

"*Carpe diem*," Amber agreed.

Lydia didn't press the issue. "You have been enjoying your stay, I hope?" she asked instead as she started to strip the massage tables.

"Very much," Amber said, grateful for the change of topic. "It's so beautiful here, and the food is amazing, and there's so much to do."

"Will you be joining us tomorrow evening at the dance?" Lydia asked.

Amber immediately imagined dancing with Tony and her breath caught. "I don't really dance," she said uncomfortably.

"I teach a class right before the dance," Lydia said coaxingly. "I can show you all of the steps you need to know."

Amber glanced over at her.

Lydia smiled innocently back.

Amber smiled back. "I'll come," she agreed.

Chapter 12

TONY COULD HAVE KICKED himself.

"Oh yes, I speak Spanish and Russian and Chinese," he mocked himself in a mutter. "Because *that* matches my cover story."

He hated that he had to continue to keep Amber in the dark about who he was, and kept ridiculously forgetting that he had told her the story he was using with the resort. It felt like he had known her forever, that she must know every one of his secrets.

Which is why he was getting Rochelle to send him the paperwork that would give him clearance to tell Amber what he was really doing there... if the WiFi would ever start working.

That was another conflict he'd had with Scarlet since his arrival. "We encourage our guests to disconnect," she had told him scathingly. "And we're on a private island off a foreign country generating all our own power; Internet reliability is not a priority. This is made clear in your rental agreement."

Tony wondered if there was more to it than that. It certainly was down at perfectly inconvenient times.

"It'll be in your inbox," Rochelle assured him. "And I promise not to breathe a word to Rick."

When he spotted Amber later, sitting on the bar deck over-looking the pool, it was like coming home. *Soon,* he thought. *Soon I'll be able to honestly talk about a* future *with her.*

She smiled and waved at him. "Want to get some food?" she asked, standing to greet him with a shy kiss.

"It's still a while before dinner is served," Tony said, auto-matically checking the spot on his wrist where his watch used to be. "But I could use some food now, too."

Amber slipped her hand into his as they walked, and he gratefully kept it; there was something satisfying about having even that tiny amount of contact between them.

The buffet had been replenished and freshened since they'd last been there. Both of them took heaping tacos that bore only a passing resemblance to their American fast food cousins, and ate them with relish and mess, licking their fingers and plates with laughter.

Amber took a glass of wine with her second plate. "I'm on vacation," she said defiantly.

"Don't have to defend yourself to me!" Tony chuckled. He took a beer, and they lingered over their drinks until the wait-staff began to set the tables for dinner and the sun began its journey to setting over the water.

"I haven't been to the beach yet," Amber said as they left the dining hall and paused at an intersection of the paths. Some-thing in her voice suggested to Tony that she wasn't really inter-ested in a walk.

"You aren't missing much," Tony said off-handedly. "Lots of sand, some crabs, maybe a dead fish."

Amber's eyes sparkled back at him. "I'm sure you have a much better idea?"

"There's a fine view of the sunset from my cottage porch," he purred at her.

TONY WOKE WITH AMBER snuggled so naturally in his arms that he wondered how he'd ever slept without her.

"Did my stomach wake you up?" she asked with a giggle as it gave another hungry rumble.

They had skipped dinner in favor of talking about nothing and making slow love late into the night. His deck had a better view than Amber's did, and they sat on the loveseat watching the stars creep across the sky, fingers entwined, her sweet, strong body curled up close beside him.

Tony's stomach gave an answering growl. "I think it was my own stomach that woke me," he admitted.

The sun was rising over the resort and the sky was already light; they hadn't closed the curtains the night before, or the sliding doors. The surf was loud against the shore and there were birds crying in the jungle.

"We're in time to catch breakfast," Amber suggested, and it became a laughing race for clothes, hindered by tickling and kissing.

Their bellies were still giving a chorus of need when they arrived at the restaurant, and a grinning waiter who introduced himself as Breck seated them overlooking the bar deck and pool below. He brought them coffee with a flirtatious wink at Tony.

"What are your plans for the day?" Amber asked, sipping the froth from the top of her coffee drink.

Tony frowned, thinking about the dead-end he'd run into on his mission. He ought to be taking it more seriously, putting more pressure on the infuriating Scarlet, or pursuing more staff interviews. It was easy to forget he was at the resort on business; Amber seemed to drive all other thoughts from his mind.

"I was thinking about taking a yoga class later this morning," Amber suggested when Tony was silent. "Would you like to join me?"

"I have some... er... work from the office I should do today," Tony said awkwardly. He hated every word of the lie.

Amber smiled at him indulgently. "That's okay," she said understandingly, possibly thinking that he felt yoga was too unmanly for him.

"There's a dance tonight," Tony remembered. "At the event hall. Some kind of formal affair with a live salsa band."

"Oh, I saw that," Amber said, and Tony thought she looked a little wistful. "Lydia told me there's a dance class right before it to teach the basic steps."

"Would you care to attend with me, my lady?" Tony asked chivalrously. "I packed a suit for the occasion."

Amber's eyes glowed. "I would very much like that," she said shyly. "But I will definitely need to take the dance class beforehand."

"I will join you for that," Tony promised. "Leave space in your dance card for me."

Amber smiled and blushed in delight. "I will endeavor to do so," she teased.

Then Breck brought them plates of fluffy, cheese-smothered omelets with perfect toast and fresh fruit bowls and spread napkins in their laps. Conversation was forgotten in the need to fill their empty stomachs.

After a breakfast that had them both groaning and happily holding their sides, Tony gave Amber a swift kiss and she went to find the yoga class, protesting that she would be incapable of bending into the poses.

From the deck above, Tony discovered that Scarlet was at the bar; she appeared to be having a heated discussion with Jimmy, the lifeguard, and one of the handymen. Tony's eyes narrowed, wondering how long that would keep her, then swiftly turned and left by the back restaurant exit, taking the turn uphill towards her office.

He stopped at the Y in the path that split off to the spa and took a small device from his pocket. It separated into two pieces, and he tucked one into his ear, placing the other carefully beside the path to resort entrance. He walked past it twice to test the range and was satisfied that it would only alarm for someone choosing the path towards the courtyard.

He moved quietly, swiftly, and was relieved to find that the structure at the top of the resort was quiet and empty. They were far enough from the ocean that the sound of the plants rustling in the wind was louder here than the surf.

He prowled around first the outside, then the inside perimeter of the building. It was basically a large, square donut, with storage and utility rooms along three sides, Scarlet's office and what appeared to be a large bedroom suite on the downhill side looking out over the resort. There was a small, private lawn that opened off of it, and a patio with a table and a single chair.

Her office door was open to the inner courtyard, which Tony found odd. As private as the woman was, she seemed like the door-shut sort of person. His interview with her had been frustrating and useless; she asked him as many questions as he'd managed to ask her.

He went in carefully, scanning for alarm systems or electronics, and found nothing. A laptop sitting open on the desk was the most modern device in the room, everything else was clearly from the 80s when the resort was first built. Locking filing cabinets surrounded the window behind her desk, and potted plants filled most of the windowsill. The room had tall bookshelves on two sides, and one wall held a map of the resort half-shrouded in the trailing vines that looped all around the room. Tony left the laptop alone; he didn't have a warrant—yet—and everything that he could do legally should be done first.

He went to the closest bookshelf and scanned titles.

Like the décor, there was nothing more recent than the 80s, and every book looked well-read. He took out his phone and started taking photos of the spines. Rochelle might be able to come up with some kind of pattern in the titles, but he could not. There were foreign language books, several books on management and accounting, a range of classical literature, the complete Encyclopedia Britannica, books on botany and gardening, on mythical creatures, on maintaining small engines... and an entire row of Georgette Heyer. Not all of them were in English.

Tony took a book out at random, a book of Swedish to English, and found that it had tidy notations and cross-references in the edges.

He was just putting it back when the hairs at the back of his neck rose.

"Can I *help* you?"

Scarlet's voice—with him, at least—was always rather chilly, but Tony felt like the temperature in the room had just fallen ten degrees.

"The door was open," he growled, turning to face her.

She didn't look amused. "Most people are *polite* enough not to snoop through what is clearly a private office."

Tony scowled at her, feeling like he'd just been scolded by a teacher. A very severe teacher. "I was waiting for you," he lied. "My agency assures me that they've sent everything you asked for."

"Our service provider on the mainland has been having technical difficulties," Scarlet said tightly. "They assure me that our data should resume at full strength within the next day or two. I'm sure whatever has been sent will be here shortly."

"Awfully convenient," Tony muttered.

Scarlet's eyes flashed, but she didn't protest the accusation. "If there's anything else I can help you with?" she asked tightly.

There wasn't.

"Thank you for your time," Tony ground out.

"You're very *welcome*," Scarlet said with exactly the same measure of sincerity.

She stepped aside, arms folded over her chest, and Tony left with his chin high and his temper higher.

The blare of the alarm in his ear surprised him, and he crouched into a fighting stance before he realized that he'd set off his own proximity alert. He went back two paces and picked the device out of the brush he'd put it in, staring at it curiously. How had she managed to get past without triggering it? The only other ways up into the courtyard involved hiking through the jungle or hopping over the wall that edged the top of the resort... and Tony couldn't imagine the terribly proper Scarlet doing either of these things.

He returned to his cottage and found that the bed had been made and the room straightened. He sat down with his laptop to jot down notes from the unproductive interview and download the photos, glancing at his phone and frowning to find that the WiFi was still down.

Chapter 13

AMBER ARRIVED AT THE event hall self-consciously smoothing down her sundress. It was not all that fancy, but it felt flirty. She hoped it wouldn't be too out of place.

Lydia greeted her cheerfully, dressed in a splashy red dress. The flirtatious waiter from the restaurant, Breck, was there as well, already walking slowly through the steps with a white-haired woman who was blushing and smiling at his attention.

Only a handful of people showed up for the class, Tony last and most importantly of all. Amber mistrusted the way her heart sped up and her belly clenched at the sight of him. She had hoped that the day apart would remind her that this was just a vacation fling, just a temporary, whirlwind affair that would be over with the week that was galloping by too quickly.

But his smile when he caught sight of her left her breathless, before he even stooped to give her a quick, possessive kiss.

It wasn't the kiss of a casual fling, it was a confident, warm kiss, with layers of expectation and promises of more.

But that was impossible, wasn't it? They were only living their short, false fantasies for a short time.

Tony, unlike Amber, had no need of the class and was clearly already comfortable with the step-step-step-pause rhythm of salsa. Lydia pulled him to the front of the class and used him to demonstrate the steps. Amber, terribly distracted by how incredible Tony looked in a suit, trod on Breck's toes a dozen time.

He grinned at her. "You found yourself a beautiful mate at our resort," he observed near her ear. "Step back."

Amber stepped forward and clashed her knee against his. "Oh, oops," she said, blushing. Mate seemed like an odd word to choose; Breck didn't sound English or Australian.

"The other back," Breck teased. "Step forward this time!"

She concentrated on her feet and the dance pattern with determination and made a successful circle around the room with the waiter before he led her to where Tony was dutifully practicing with the white-haired woman and switched partners with a knowing wink.

"You're really good at this," Amber told Tony breathlessly.

"You're beautiful," he told her, and Amber found herself drowning in his eyes.

There was a short break after the class while the band set up. They walked out to watch twilight falling over the cliffs and the ocean swirling beyond.

"After this week..." Tony started to say.

But there was no 'after this week' that Amber wanted to think about and she swiftly changed the topic. "Can you believe the view? Pictures don't even do it justice. I wish there was a way to hold onto the whole thing... the smell, and the sounds, and the heat, all of it." *You*, she didn't add.

Tony didn't press the issue, only agreed with her, and they talked inanely about the perfect weather and the beauties of the jungle, standing close together, fingers entwined.

The band began to play and they walked back through the gathering dark to the event hall, which had been transformed;

it had seemed dim compared to the fierce daylight, and now it was brilliant in the surrounding darkness, filled with happy music and a gathering of satisfied guests and attentive staff.

Amber had been to dances in high school; they had been unmitigated hell. She'd been filled with longing for a connection, any connection, and had been rebuffed, sometimes even teased. She was an orphan, in a small town where everyone had family, and had been unfriendly and cold in an attempt to protect her sensitive heart. It didn't surprise her that no one wanted to dance with her, or be her friend, it only reinforced her suspicion that she was unlovable and undesirable.

But this night, this was everything her teenage self had ever dreamed of.

Tony danced every dance with her, and she was distantly aware that they were the focus of many amused and envious glances. He was tall and utterly dreamy, and Amber found it difficult to believe that *she* was the one in his arms.

They didn't talk, to Amber's gratitude, though they laughed often; she wanted to live this beautiful fantasy as long as she could. He made her feel light and graceful and complete as the music swelled around them, and it wasn't until much much later that Amber realized that her legs were aching and her feet were complaining.

"Can I get you a drink?" he offered.

She already felt drunk, Amber thought. Like she was drifting through the night in a seductive haze. "Just water," she said, out of breath.

They walked to the little bar set up at the side of the dance floor.

She felt Tony stiffen at her side and realized that Scarlet was behind the bar. The woman's serene smile felt chilly compared to the warmth of her staff. "Can I get you something?" she offered politely.

"Water," Tony said briefly and Amber shot him a look. The lazy, fairy tale bubble that they had been dancing in was gone and he looked unexpectedly cold and unapproachable.

"Very well," Scarlet said just a briefly, and she poured them two glasses from a frosty pitcher, handing them over the counter without expression.

Amber's feet were hurting in earnest now, and she was grateful when Tony led them to a chair at the side of the floor.

"It's so unfair," she said, trying to lighten the mood again as she bent to take her shoes off and rub her feet. "The cutest things are always the most uncomfortable."

Tony smiled at her, and it brought back every bit of the magical moment. "Not all of the cutest things," he said, and when he leaned forward to kiss her, it wasn't anything but completely natural to kiss him back. Amber gladly forgot about the severe red-headed resort owner, and all the secrets Tony was keeping from her.

Chapter 14

TONY WAS TECHNICALLY proficient at dancing, but he'd never particularly enjoyed it... until now.

Dancing with Amber wasn't a duty, or an expectation, it was joy. She was laughing and blushing in his arms, protesting her lack of skills but gamely enjoying herself.

She was his mate, Tony thought with satisfaction, and he could imagine nothing more perfect than this dance and this entire beautiful week since she had arrived and turned his life upside down.

But every dance had to end sometime and he finally walked with her to the edge of the floor, stared Scarlet down over glasses of water, and found free seats together at the quieter end of the hall.

As much as he wanted to continue kissing her—and do other things that he was sure Scarlet would descend on like a nun with a ruler—he pulled back. "After this..." he started, not sure how to go on. "Once I'm done..."

"After this, I'm expecting you to take me back to your cottage," Amber said, neatly deflecting the conversation about the future again.

Tony didn't have permission to tell her anything yet anyway. "Another turn around the floor first?"

"Not in these cute shoes," Amber said, her golden eyes laughing.

They rose to their feet and wandered out into the velvet night, Amber barefoot.

"Do you want me to carry you?" Tony offered, when they got to a place where the smooth white concrete turned to gravel.

"That's ridiculous," she said, giggling, but she didn't protest when he scooped her up and carried her the final steps into his cottage.

He put her down on the bed, kicking the door closed behind him, and kissed her passionately as she tossed her shoes across the room.

But it wasn't the same way that they had kissed before, and it wasn't the same ardor that had driven their previous lovemaking. She held his face as she kissed him, in no hurry to undress him, lingering over removing every layer.

Tony took his cues from her and they slowed, spending extra moments with lazy caresses and gentle, brushing kisses.

He knew her, so completely, in so short a time. He *knew* the touches that would make her breath hitch, and the places that made her eyes close in pleasure.

Everything felt different. It felt... like she was trying to memorize him, like she was trying to stretch each precious moment as long as possible.

Like she wasn't ready to say goodbye...

"Amber," Tony said quietly, when they lay together afterwards, a single sheet over them to keep the evening chill off.

Her breathing was slow and even.

"I... love you."

But she was already asleep.

A SHARP RAP ON THE door woke him.

Disoriented, Tony sat upright in bed, grasping at empty covers in the space where Amber had been. Sunlight spilled around the corners of the curtains, and he could see in the light that her clothing was gone; there was no trace of her anywhere. He rolled out of bed and staggered out of the bedroom as the knocking was repeated, more impatiently than before.

"I'm coming," he roared, and he nearly paused for the bathrobe before deciding that it served whoever it was right to meet them naked at the door.

Scarlet, dressed in a perfectly crisp linen skirt suit, looked entirely unfazed by his nudity.

Of course, Tony realized with chagrin. She did run a clothing-optional resort, after all. He, on the other hand, would have appreciated having a layer of clothing to give him some shreds of dignity. He settled for a dark scowl, crossing his big arms at her. "What do you want?"

"It's not what I want," Scarlet said, all business. "It's what you've been hounding me for all week." She thrust a file folder at him, all but forcing it into his hands. "I've cleared your background," she said, no hint of apology in her voice for her earlier obstruction.

"About time," Tony said gruffly, recognizing his own lack of graciousness. He opened the file folder to flip briefly through a stack of xeroxed forms, one for each of the missing shifters. He suspiciously wondered if Scarlet had purposefully delayed long enough to falsify the information she was giving him; there was something secretive about the woman that challenged his trust.

"You're *welcome*," Scarlet said coldly, and she turned on her heel and stalked away with a click of heels on concrete.

Tony shut the door behind her a little harder than he meant to, and crossed the room to the desk. He tapped a finger on the file folder, then looked through the open door to the bedroom with a furrow in his brow.

It bothered him that Amber was gone. It was deeply unsettling that she had been able to leave without waking him, and it gave him a pang of worry that she had *wanted* to.

Maybe she had just gotten hungry, and hadn't wished to wake him? It was mid-morning, maybe she was generally an early riser. Tony tried to find some peace in the idea, and failed to.

As much as he wanted to immediately go find her, he decided instead to get dressed, and get back to the job at hand.

He had work to do.

Chapter 15

THE SUNRISE, PEEKING in through the gaps in the curtains, had pried Amber's eyes open, and she crept out of Tony's cottage using all the cat-silent skills she'd honed as a teenager. Tony barely stirred as she dressed herself, and she carefully latched the front door behind her, smiling to remember how it had gaped open while they made enthusiastic love their first night.

She had certainly taken her intention to have fun seriously. Her smile felt brittle, as she remembered that her time here would end altogether too soon, and she'd be saying goodbye to the big, charming man who had captured her heart.

The walk to her cottage felt impossibly steep and lonely, and she showered swiftly.

She put on a clean pair of shorts and a plain babydoll t-shirt that flattered her curves but wasn't as revealing as the shirt of the previous night and finished the look with a pair of low wedge sandals. She paused to look at her reflection, and grimaced at herself. Her long dark hair and slightly dusky skin could have been anything—Hispanic, perhaps, or Middle Eastern. Someone had once told her she looked Native American, and another had suggested east Indian. Her brown eyes were strangely light and golden, and her cheekbones not quite right for any specific nationality. Her diminutive height suggested Asian, but the shape of her eyes did not.

Maybe South American, like her animal form? Amber pushed the idea away. She certainly wasn't going to figure out her origins here, as she had half-hoped she might. She didn't look like any of the Costa Ricans she had met, and no one had ever heard of an Andean mountain cat shifter.

Her stomach reminded her that dinner had been very early the previous night, before a great deal of activity.

A sign at the dining hall door reminded visitors that clothing was required for establishments serving hot food, and there was a rack of bathrobes, in case someone was caught by surprise.

"Chef has something special on deck for breakfast this morning," Breck promised suggestively, winking at Amber as he pulled out the chair for her, and then spread a napkin in her lap.

"Chef," it turned out, was a distinguished older man who cared enough about his clientele to come out and check with her halfway through the exquisite meal.

"I've never had souffle before," Amber confessed to him. "And until today, I would have not guessed that I liked artichokes."

Chef looked ridiculously pleased. "The secret is fresh eggs and good cream," he said proudly. "The bacon crumbles don't hurt anything," he added conspiratorially.

Amber indulged in a second plate, with a side of fresh fruit pieces and another cup of strong, dark coffee.

Her table gave her a wonderful view of the dining area, and she people-watched shamelessly, enjoying the way that Breck doted on his customers, and how friendly and cheerful the other guests were.

One woman in particular Amber had to keep herself from staring at—she had clearly been there some time and knew all of the staff by name. She held herself like a queen, confident and assured as she directed her breakfast. She was gorgeous, with loose, waist-long, auburn hair and flawless makeup, and she was also the largest woman that Amber had ever seen. She honestly wasn't sure how the woman's chair held her up, and half-expected it to crumple beneath her at one dramatic gesture of her hand.

"That's Magnolia," Breck told her, refilling her coffee. "Isn't she just a dish? She's one of our long-term residents and we all just adore her."

Embarrassed to be caught staring, Amber quickly finished off her plate and drank the last of her coffee.

She had a moment of hesitation as she left the dining hall—an odd expectation that she ought to be somewhere, doing something, and she wasn't sure what that was.

"You're on vacation," she reminded herself. Most of her wanted to scamper straight back to Tony's cottage. But she didn't want to appear too desperate or clingy. *Just a vacation fling,* she told herself firmly. She turned her sandaled feet past the pool and down to the beach.

The winding stone paths led her to one edge of a long crescent beach, bright sand edged with emerald green shrubbery on one side and sapphire blue ocean on the other. She passed a cottage being renovated by two shirtless men who lent support to her theory about Scarlet's employment requirements including modeling. She smirked to compare them in her mind to Tony's gorgeous physique, then scolded herself for thinking about him again.

The beach had a collection of comfortable chairs, and a small open structure that held a tiny bar (with no bartender in sight), piles of fluffy beach towels, and an array of sunscreen bottles. There were even a few pairs of sunglasses and hats in various sizes. There were sturdy umbrellas, spaced along the beach. At the far end of the beach was a dock, where a sailboat was moored across from a larger boat with a Shifting Sands logo on the side.

But what made Amber stop and stare, gape-mouthed, was the lifeguard. Curled around the guard tower was a dragon, as big and real as life, gleaming green and gold in the early sun. She might have guessed it was some crazy jeweled sculpture, but it swiveled a long mobile face towards her, and blinked curiously at her twice before returning its gaze to the ocean, where a few people were splashing on body boards.

A dragon!

She had heard rumors of mythical shifters, but hadn't expected to ever meet one, and now that she was faced with one, she couldn't do more than stare in shock. She felt foolish for thinking she was special for being a rare cat shifter.

After a long moment, she gathered up a towel and chair, and found a spot near the end of the beach, where the sand curved around towards the head rocks so she could surreptitiously watch the dragon while still facing the water.

She closed her eyes, drinking in the feeling of sunlight on her skin, and tried to relax to the mesmerizing sound of the waves and the wind in the jungle leaves.

She was not surprised to open her eyes and find Tony, wearing only shorts, walking over the sand towards her, his own chair and towel tucked under his arm. The leap that her heart gave in her chest was both thrilling and unwelcome.

How many times was she going to have to remind herself that this was not a real relationship? The thrill of desire that went through her body at the sight of his muscled arms and strong legs was to be expected, but she needed to keep her emotions in check, and she was doing an utterly miserable job at that.

Ours, her cat purred rapturously.

You aren't helping, Amber replied.

"You left," Tony said accusingly, when he was standing right next to her. Clearly, she had violated some expectation of courtesy, in his mind.

Amber attempted to play it cool.

"I needed breakfast," she said offhandedly. "I was starving! And you know, no predation, so I figured I'd better head to the restaurant."

Tony set up the chair close enough to her that their armrests touched, and when he sat down, he took her hand and twined his fingers into hers.

"Was breakfast good?" Tony asked, tipping his head back so he could smile across at her.

Amber licked her lips in memory. "Exquisite!" she said enthusiastically. "You missed a treat."

"Alas," Tony said, with mock tragedy.

"Chef should be in a restaurant in New York City that you can't get reservations at for a week," Amber said, pretending she knew anything about high-end restaurants. "Scarlet has done an impressive job staffing this place."

She felt Tony's hand stiffen under her fingers.

"You don't like her, do you," she guessed, before she could stop herself. *None of your business, stupid,* she told herself.

"I don't trust her," Tony said. "She's been... obstructionist."

Amber tipped down her sunglasses and looked at him. "You're not really here for vacation," she said finally.

Tony squirmed.

"I'm sorry," Amber said swiftly, loosening her fingers so he could pull free if he wanted. "You don't have to tell me. It can be just a vacation if you want."

But Tony squeezed her back. "I'm part of a top secret government agency, Shifter Affairs, and I'm here as part of an investigation."

Amber blinked at him, but somehow wasn't as surprised as she thought she ought to be. And most of her was relieved that at least he wasn't *married.* "What are you investigating?" she asked.

Tony seemed to relax a little, the beach chair groaning a little as he settled. "Shifters have been going missing from this resort in particular for the past several years—sometimes they vanish on their way here, sometimes after they've checked out. One was mysteriously lost at sea during their stay, no body found. It's all been going on almost as long as Scarlet has been here. There's some thought that another government entity was poaching potential agents, but I think something more sinister is happening; the missing people don't all fit the profile."

"And you think Scarlet might have something to do with it?" The idea was chilling. More chilling: "And there's a government agency that knows about shifters? As in, the American government?"

"It's more like a... an... international x-file agency," Tony floundered. "That happens to know about shifters. We deal with all sorts of weird cases, but they aren't all shifters."

Amber glanced down the beach at the dragon who was still attentively watching the swimmers. "Is there a... registry?" She was sitting up in her chair now, all attention and no part relaxation. "Are they worried about... I don't know, an uprising, or a shifter revolution? Should we worry about being on a *list*?" Bad movie plots flitted through her head.

"Nothing like that." Tony shook his head with confidence. "Most shifters are peaceful and perfectly legal. We only deal with the criminal elements, and our records aren't public."

"Ooo," Amber couldn't help saying. "Criminal elements! You're like a James Bond superspy, aren't you!"

"But with a lot more paperwork and a lot less flying burning helicopters and disarming bombs," Tony laughed.

Amber laughed, then sobered and bit her lip. "You said you have *records*," she said, not sure how to proceed.

Tony was not oblivious to her train of thought, following her line of questioning to its logical conclusion. "You want to know if there are more Andean mountain cats, like you. Maybe your parents."

"I'm sure it's not as important as shifters disappearing today," Amber said, heart in her mouth. She gave a dry laugh. "And I have to *hope* they aren't on the wrong side of the law." But if they were, would that explain why they gave her up?

The combination of the idea, and Tony's intoxicating closeness, made her feel dizzy and unsettled. *Just a vacation fling,* she wanted to scream at herself.

"I can check," Tony said, making circles on the back of her hand with his thumb. "I will. If we've got any information, I'll find it for you."

Amber let the air out of her lungs all at once, not realizing that she had been holding her breath. "I'd appreciate that," she confessed in a small voice.

"It doesn't matter to me," he told her gruffly. "Where you're from, who your parents are. I don't give a damn." He looked at her so intensely, his brown eyes warm and direct. "I know who *you* are."

Amber blinked at him, overwhelmed. She could no more doubt him than doubt the air she was breathing, but it made no sense. Tony's eyes were full of promises, not empty flattery—promises of love and life together. She tried to remind herself again that this wasn't *real*, but could only see the warmth in his eyes and remember the way they had kissed and made love, and wonder if it could possibly be something more.

I don't get happy endings, she reminded herself fiercely. Too many times she had longed for stability, for family, only to have it ripped away.

James Bond never stayed with any of the Bond girls, she reminded herself. He had beautiful, casual beach flings and went away afterwards and was a spy again.

Just like Tony would.

Because that was all this was.

Right?

Amber couldn't make sense of the emotion swirling in her chest. "I have to go!" she said loudly, in terror and confusion, and she scrambled backwards out of her chair, tipping it over. She fled over the sand, stumbling and staggering over the uneven surface ungracefully.

"Amber, wait!" Tony said behind her and Amber ran faster.

The dragon lifeguard turned in alarm, hearing their commotion, but didn't uncurl itself from the lifeguard chair.

She made it back to the dining hall faster than she expected, winded by the uphill sprint, and she leaned against the stone wall panting.

"Amber!" It wasn't Tony, but Amber's alarm was no less. Jimmy was putting a cellphone in his pocket. "Your timing is perfect," he said with a big smile. "I was just organizing a tour of Mr Big's estate gardens for a few of the guests. Wouldn't you like to join us?"

His whole vibe was of a greasy salesman, but the idea was so appealing to Amber that she instantly agreed. "Yes. That is perfect. When are you leaving?"

"The van is already gassed up and ready to go," Jimmy said brightly. "Be at the resort entrance in ten minutes!"

Something about his eagerness left Amber feeling dirty, but she was too grateful for an excuse to escape to examine the feeling.

She didn't want to think about any feelings, too sure that she had made a terrible mistake in losing her heart altogether.

"Is his name really Mr. Big?" she had to ask.

Jimmy laughed. "Not *Big*," he clarified. "*Beehag*. It's an old English name."

"Ah!" Amber tried to laugh with him, but it came out very dry and humorless. She suspected the mysterious man was going to remain Mr. Big in her head for a long time.

Chapter 16

TONY WATCHED AMBER flee with confusion and dismay, not even comforted by the exciting sight of her gorgeous little ass as she ran across the sand. What had he done wrong?

Had she heard his declaration of love the night before? Was she trying to tell him that she didn't feel the same? He felt the pull of his mate at an undeniable level, but every time he got close emotionally or tried to talk about the future, she seemed to get skittish, and this time he'd managed to scare her right off.

He scrubbed a hand across his face.

He'd also managed to tell her more about his agency than he was authorized to, and knew *that* was going to be some paperwork. There were a few shifters in his chain of command who might be tolerant about the slip due to the fact that Amber was his mate, but there were others who would definitely not.

And it was going to be a tough fact to prove, given that Amber was hell-bent on running away from him.

After giving a hefty sigh, he hauled himself up out of the beach chair. A glance down the beach at the watchful dragon lifeguard convinced him to fold up both his chair and Amber's abandoned one, and haul them back to the beach shed.

Back at the cottage, he booted up his laptop and picked up the cellphone, flipping open the folder that Scarlet had given him.

The signal was spotty. If it was cloudy, he'd be out of luck, but today he had solid bars. The WiFi, on the other hand, was *still* down.

He dialed the cellphone and waited, hoping the signal held. While he waited for the connection to be made, he flipped through the paperwork for a second time, hoping to find something new in the information.

"Rick," the voice at the other end finally said with disinterest.

"Richie!" Tony said.

There was a slight satellite delay, and Richard asked, "How's Costa Rica, Tony? Is it grrrrrrreeeeeeeat?"

"Har, har," Tony said, but he expected the familiar jibe. "Hey, listen up. I don't know how long my cellphone signal will last."

"Wow, Tony, you mean you've actually gotten some work done and have information? You're not just lying on the sand in the sun flirting with pretty girls at the *clothing-optional* resort on the agency dime?"

"I got the paperwork from Scarlet, finally," Tony said, without taking the bait. "And believe me, I had to work for it."

"Did you flex your muscles for her?" Rick teased. "Make promises? *Rise* to the occasion?"

Tony bit back his desire to tell Rick about Amber. He wasn't even sure what to tell Rick—was Amber going to continue to bolt away from him like he'd offended her in some way? Was it just taking her a little time to get used to the idea of a mate? Tony shook his head and brought himself back to the conversation. The satellite delay covered his confusion.

"There's nothing very helpful here," Tony said dryly. "Notes about food allergies and preferences, what activities they attended, what shifter type they were. Nothing seems to tie them together at all—they are all different kinds of animals, from different places. Some of them attended morning yoga, some of them didn't. One was allergic to peanuts."

"We can put it in a database and feed it to Rochelle," Rick suggested. "She can pick patterns out of nothing."

Tony was squinting at the pages. "Yeah," he said, distracted by a sudden thought. "I'll scan these and set them to email as soon as I've got WiFi or data again."

"Send me photos, too," Rick laughed. "Selfies that happen to have good beach babes in the background would be preferred. Clothing *optional*."

Tony licked his lips. "Look, I have a favor to ask."

"One worth a great selfie from the beach? Maybe one that doesn't happen to have you in it?"

"I'll send you a dozen," Tony promised, smiling to think of getting the dragon in the shot, or the English boar couple who liked to bask in the sand in animal form.

"What's the favor?"

"I'm looking for a person, maybe a couple, on the run. One of them might have been an Andean mountain cat. They would have passed through Lakefield, about twenty-six years ago."

Tony heard Rick typing. The sound was strangely tinny over the poor connection.

"Lakefield Ontario, or Lakefield Minnesota?" Rick asked.

"Minnesota, I'd guess." She had a Midwestern accent and loved casserole, Tony thought. It was outrageous that he could know someone as intensely as he knew Amber and not even know if she was American or Canadian. "Look for a church called Saint Mary's. A baby was dropped there."

"Who happened to be an Andean mountain cat shifter," Rick guessed. "I've never even heard of an Andean mountain cat. Pretty, aren't they!" He must have looked it up on the Internet while they were talking.

Tony thought about Amber's petite, lush form, and her incredible golden-brown eyes. "You have no idea," he said. His thoughts were starting to form into a pattern.

"Pretty and... rare." He picked up the paperwork in front of him again, sifting through the pages with a fresh outlook. "One of these missing shifters was a white tiger," Tony said thoughtfully. "And one was a sand cat."

"You don't see many of those," Rick agreed.

"Another was a Borneo bay cat, and here's a Northern quoll." Tony said, unease rising in his throat as he skimmed faster, flipping through the pages, now with a specific field in mind.

"A what?"

Tony wasn't sure if Rick didn't know what a quoll was, or if he hadn't heard over the static on the line. "A quoll," he repeated. "It's an Australian marsupial." He wouldn't have known that himself, if it hadn't been noted on the form.

"I'm starting to see a pattern," Rick said.

"*Rare*. All of the missing shifters are *rare*."

"Like someone's... collecting them?"

"*Amber,*" Tony said, ice in his throat. He dropped the phone, not even sure if he'd hung it up first, and bolted for the door. The files spilled off the desk behind him, but he didn't stop.

Chapter 17

"A FEW OF THE GUESTS" proved to be just three other people—the English boar couple who turned up their noses at Amber's sandy sandals and simple tank top, and a flinty-eyed man who spoke Spanish with Jimmy without acknowledging Amber's presence.

Nothing less than grateful for his company to spare her Jimmy's attention, Amber went for an empty seat in the far back of the van, even knowing that the bumps would be the worst there. She had a bottle of water, her phone in her pocket, and a straw hat—courtesy of the resort—to keep the worst of the sun from her face.

Most of the drive was through thick jungle, over a rain-pitted road that wandered seemingly randomly through gullies and along ridges, further than Amber would have guessed possible on an island of finite size. She had drained half her bottle by the time the road finally resolved into a driveway and passed through a set of heavy iron gates. To her surprise, there were guards at the gate, each carrying a formidable-looking rifle.

Maybe Mr. Big—Mr. *Beehag*—just really liked his privacy.

The van drove past the very large house to a second structure, much more modest, and Amber was happy to escape from the deafening metal box and stretch her legs again. She was glad for her hat here; the jungle had been cleared a good distance around the estate—which looked more like a compound to her eyes—and the sun was beating down. They were higher than she thought they would be, and she could see far out over the jungle, to the distant ocean beyond and below.

Mr Beehag proved to be younger than Amber had expected of an island-owning eccentric billionaire, with a quick smile that showed perfect white teeth. The teeth seemed odd paired with the sophisticated English accent. Amber couldn't help but compare him unfavorably with Tony and then wanted to kick herself for thinking about him again.

Surprisingly, he all but ignored the English couple, who introduced themselves as the Bellinghams, and took Amber's hand.

"Welcome to my arboretum," he said smoothly. To her be-fuddlement, he kissed it. "You would be Amber, and you must call me Alistair." It wasn't so much a suggestion as a command.

"Alright," Amber said, raising eyebrows at him. "Alistair, then. Thank you for having us here."

She tried to include the others in her statement, but found that Jimmy and the Spanish-speaking man had both vanished.

The English boar couple looked unimpressed, but made vague polite noises.

"I assure you, the pleasure is mine!" Alistair's smile was dis-tractingly white, and anything but vague.

Something about the way he looked at her made the tiny hairs at the back of Amber's neck rise, and she was glad when he led them all to the doors of the arboretum and unlocked them at a very modern-looking keypad.

The arboretum, at least, was everything that Jimmy had promised, and Amber was just as happy that he didn't reappear while Alistair showed them around.

The eccentric billionaire was an educated host, and he knew all of the plants in his collection. He had entertaining stories about most of them, and was clearly proud of some of the very exotic and rare flowers he had convinced to blossom.

Amber quickly forgot how oddly attentive he was, and found herself in easy conversation about fertilizer choices and the use of blooming chemicals. Costa Rica had a reputation for ecotourism and going organic, and Amber couldn't help but approve of the fact that Alistair was following that trend.

They were standing at the base of what Alistair insisted was one of the rarest palm varieties in the world when Amber realized that she hadn't noticed the other couple in an unusually long time—and also, she was starving! The sun was just beginning to descend towards the ocean.

"Did we lose the Bellinghams?" she asked. "And goodness, I should be getting back to the resort for dinner..." Her water was long since gone; she had been using the empty bottle to keep her hands from fidgeting for some time.

"I am a shameful host," Alistair said, with a glint in his eyes that made Amber suspect nothing was an accident. "We bored the Bellinghams back to the resort some hours ago; Jimmy took them. You must stay to supper with me while he returns, and I will show you the rest of my collection."

Amber's curiosity was piqued; they had passed several sets of electronically locked doors that she had wondered about, and the walls were all much higher than privacy on a private island really required.

"I..." she thought about Tony; was he wondering where she was?

I don't owe him anything, she told herself fiercely. *It isn't a real relationship.*

He hadn't even been honest about his profession, at first. But she couldn't help but remember his face as he told her she was beautiful, and the way his thumb made circles on her hand.

"I'd love to have dinner," she said firmly.

Chapter 18

TONY SPRINTED FOR AMBER's cottage, and when he found a locked door, knocked ferociously.

"Amber!" he called. "Amber, answer me!"

When she didn't, he circled the place, and easily climbed onto the porch without resorting to shifting. His tiger roared for release, but he was a little afraid of the intensity of the fear mounting in his chest. The curtains on the big glass doors were pulled back, and the rooms inside were dark and empty. Unless Amber was cowering in the bathroom...

She is not, his tiger snarled at him.

He stalked back along the path, first trying the dining hall, then the pool. He didn't want to believe the tiger inside, who was insisting that Amber wasn't here, that she wasn't anywhere nearby. He stood at the upper entrance of the dining hall, breathing in the delicious scent of whatever Chef had invented for dinner and hating his helplessness.

Scarlet.

Scarlet would know where his mate was. Tony wasn't sure if Scarlet was behind the disappearances or not, but he knew to the bottom of his soul that she had secrets, and that she knew whatever was going on within the borders of her resort.

The path to Scarlet's office was half steps and half steep path, and he nearly collided with a curvy woman in jeans and cowboy boots who made Amber look diminutive but still barely came to Tony's shoulder. She was carrying her own luggage and she was on a cellphone.

"Jenna," the blonde was saying with vinegar. "Their mother, Jenna Bruin. Don't make me fly from Costa Rica to set you straight. Those are my kids, and if I have to, that *is* what I will do. You will not enjoy it if I end up leaving my vacation because of your incompetence, and your school will not be happy with the lawsuit I slap you with, so I suggest that you get it fixed immediately."

She was clearly enraged, and Tony's already activated tiger recognized the riled-up bear barely contained behind her fair skin. They glared at each other a long heartbeat on the path while whoever was at the other end of the phone sputtered and folded like a wet paper towel, and Tony, with gritted teeth, took himself carefully around her on the narrow walkway.

Even he wasn't going to mess with an enraged momma bear.

Scarlet was sitting behind her desk, frowning at paperwork with a familiar expression, and she didn't paste on a customer service smile when Tony burst into her close office without knocking.

"Can I help you?" she asked acidly.

"Where's Amber?"

Scarlet didn't even blink in surprise, only narrowed her eyes a small amount and gave Tony an appraising look. "She left with a group of visitors for a tour of the arboretum at the Beehag estate."

"How long ago?" Tony glanced at his wrist, and realized he still wasn't wearing a watch. Scarlet didn't have any clocks up in her office.

"About five hours ago," Scarlet said without having to check. "They should be back right about now." She was all business, green eyes narrow and thoughtful.

Tony wanted to break something, destroy Scarlet's office or smash something valuable. It would serve the woman right if he unleashed his furious tiger right now.

It took all of his restraint to instead grind out, "Where?!" and let Scarlet, moving infuriatingly slowly, lead him out to the front gates of the resort.

The van was pulling up just as they got there, and Tony didn't even have to watch the British couple climb out. He knew Amber wasn't there as surely as he knew that the sky was above him. Jimmy, on the other hand, was there, getting out of the driver's seat as if nothing at all in the world was amiss when everything in the world clearly was.

It was only a few steps around the ugly van, and Tony could pull Jimmy the rest of the way out of the driver's seat by the lapels.

"Where. Is. Amber?" he demanded through bared teeth.

Keeping his tiger inside was like trying to keep a hurricane in a bottle.

Jimmy, all big eyes and clearly rising panic, stammered, "She was invited to dinner with Mr. Beehag. I was just told to drive these nice folks back to the resort."

The boar couple was clinging to each other, staring at the conflict with big, alarmed eyes. The gardener had materialized from nowhere and was watching them with a dark look, and a handyman who had been working on the stonework stopped his work to observe in interest and alarm.

"I will kill you if she is even the tiniest bit hurt." Tony said the words through bared teeth, very close to Jimmy's face, aware that he was holding most of the man's weight in his clenched fists.

"I swear," Jimmy wept. "I was just told to drive these people back, that's all I know!"

Lies! Tony's tiger insisted.

Jimmy changed underneath his fist into a squirming, snarling weasel, all clashing, razor-sharp teeth as his clothing fell away in Tony's hands.

Just as fast, Tony was changing, his clothing ripping from the striped fur and Jimmy's clothing shredded before his claws. The weasel was ripping at his front legs, all teeth and claws and crazed frenzy, and Tony swiped at him with a paw and missed as it swarmed at his face, snapping teeth across his sensitive nose.

Before he could react, Scarlet was moving forward with more speed than she ought to have in human form and she had the weasel by the scruff of the neck. Then she was suddenly holding a very naked, terrified-looking Jimmy with one hand at his neck as if he was no more than a misbehaving schoolboy.

"You!" she said ferociously. "I will deal with you myself!"

She met Tony's eyes and Tony could not figure out what animal he was seeing there, beyond sheer power. "You will go faster through the jungle than the road. Follow the ridge east. The estate is on the opposite side of the island."

Without pausing, Tony was off, every muscle of his huge tiger body tensing with one purpose: to rescue his mate. Behind him, he heard Jimmy whimper in fear.

Chapter 19

AMBER FELT UNDER-DRESSED before she even walked in the ornate double doors to Alistair's house. The armed guards flanking the doors made her feel even more uncertain. It seemed sort of odd that there were so many of them.

The foyer was as big as her entire cottage and decorated with things that Amber immediately recognized as valuable and couldn't deny were tasteful. It was like a museum; clearly tailored to Alistair's personal taste for the rare and unique. Antique masks lined the walls, as well as colonial-era paintings that Amber felt like she ought to recognize. The furniture was all rich, solid wood, beautifully carved and subtly stained; Amber guessed that Alistair had never even seen the inside of an Ikea store.

She paused. A stairway led off to her right, curving up to a second floor. The dining room was open to the left, a decadent-smelling meal already laid out on a table long enough to run footraces.

"I'm not sure I should..." she stumbled, gesturing to her dirty sandals and worn shorts.

"My *dear*," said Alistair, and his hand at her elbow felt a little tight. "I insist. You are my... *guest*."

Amber went, because she didn't know how to deny what she tried to tell herself was a request. Although she could sense Alistair's interest in her, she didn't want to encourage it... and she wasn't sure how to discourage it politely. He wasn't like Jimmy, leering and making her feel dirty, but there was an uneasiness in Amber's stomach that she wasn't sure he deserved. Maybe it was just because she kept comparing him to Tony, and no one could measure up.

"Alright," she said, and she let the billionaire lead her to the table and pull out her chair. He even put her napkin in her lap. Maybe it was a Costa Rican custom, she wondered, thinking back to her breakfast service.

Breakfast had been very, very long ago, and when the servant put a plate of artfully arranged lampchops and tender vegetables before her, she fell into it eagerly.

"Your arboretum is amazing," she said, as her eating politely allowed. "I have never seen such an extensive collection of rare plants."

"It is charming to have someone who is enthused about it," Alistair said with an artful laugh, clearly enjoying his own food. "You are a botanist, then?"

Amber laughed. "I studied botany in college," she explained. "But mostly I just work in a garden shop. A very *rural* garden shop, where most people are concerned with strains of corn and pest control by the barrel. The most excitement I get is building hanging baskets of flowers in the spring. When it comes to exotics, all I get are aloe and jade plants. I love to read about things that grow in this climate, but I am a rank amateur when it comes to this stuff!"

"You undersell yourself," Alistair said, with a strange smile. "I find you very knowledgeable, and a delightful conversationalist."

Amber blinked at him and mumbled some shy thanks. Had she conversed all that much?

A servant took her plate, and she was startled into looking up at him. He seemed an awfully... military looking person to be waiting on a table with a towel over his arm, with short cropped hair and a thick, muscled neck.

"Dessert?" Alistair offered. "I believe the chef has prepared a *crème brule.*"

But the meal felt odd in Amber's stomach. She felt like her cat was on her metaphorical shoulders, every strand of fur on end, shrieking warnings in her ears.

"No, thank you! I'm... uh, on a diet. We really should call Jimmy to come collect me. I've imposed on you so much already."

"Let me show you the study and the private collection before you leave. It will take Jimmy some time to get back with the van," Alistair said, so mildly and logically that Amber couldn't figure out how to protest it.

She took his offered hand, and wasn't sure it was only politeness that prompted her to try to act enthused about it.

The study was a shock that took all of her acting ability to hide.

Taxidermied animals and pelts filled the cavernous room. A tiger's skin sprawled across a portion of the floor, and Amber thought immediately of Tony. There was a thick-maned lion hide in front of the fireplace.

"My grandfather's collection," Alistair said, unsettlingly close to her ear. "Of course that was colonial times, when the hunt wasn't illegal, and many of these weren't even endangered. People would even say it was immoral, but times were very different then."

"Of course," Amber said weakly.

"Come, this is not what I really wanted you to see."

He led her through the dim room, and Amber tried not to startle at the soul-less gaze of a stuffed gazelle, or the bear caught mid-roar beside it.

Alistair unlocked a sturdy wooden door with another keypad, and led her out into the warm night air. The dining room had not had windows, so Amber was surprised to realize that it was quite late. Crickets and frogs made a now-familiar drone, and a silvery moon hung in a field of glittering stars. Far away, a seabird cried hauntingly and went still.

They walked into a garden, edged with very tall fencing that after a moment, Amber recognized as cages. She was alarmed, but not as surprised as she should have been, when two guards from the door fell in step behind her.

"Much of my collection is nocturnal," Alistair said, and Amber could hear the excited pride in his voice. This was something he very much wanted to share with her, and it filled her with dread.

The first enclosure, a landscaped habitat with artful trees and a little hill with lounging rocks, proved to hide a small, agile ocelot, who jumped down from a branch to stare at them from behind the metal mesh. Amber, looking back at it, felt an odd connection. Maybe it was because she felt like she was being trapped as surely as it was.

"My father was the one who started this collection," Alistair said, leading her further down the path. "He recognized the limitations of taking the skins of these... animals, and began trapping them instead."

"You've continued his legacy, then," Amber said, trying to keep conversation casual. The next animal was a pacing tiger, white and black stripes rippling over agitated muscle. It roared as they walked past; Alistair gave no time to pause and observe. They passed a spotted deer that Amber didn't recognize, and a glass enclosure of little, thick-furred mammals. Each enclosure was carefully crafted for its residents. Amber was reminded of the best zoos.

"I've improved upon it," Alistair said proudly. "I've found some of the rarest and most precious animals, most of them just in the last few years. We've got a Borneo Bay cat," he said, his British accent pronounced. "Have you ever seen one?"

"I haven't," Amber admitted reluctantly. She was aware that her steps were slowing, and that her surreptitious glances for an exit or escape were becoming less subtle than she could wish.

"They aren't the rarest cat," Alistair said leadingly, and Amber couldn't hide her terror any longer. She came to a stop, and turned to find that only one of the guards behind her had his gun at ready. The other had a long-handled dog-catcher.

"Oh?" she said, incapable of anything more clever.

"I've been looking for an Andean mountain cat for a very long time," he said seductively. "And I think you'll be very happy in the enclosure I've made for you."

"Those skins in the study," Amber said with a sudden sick feeling in the pit of her stomach. "Were those all shifters?"

"Of course!" Alistair said in that accent that Amber couldn't hear as anything but terrifying now. "What sport is there in normal animals?"

She was spared having to answer that by a sudden, blaring alarm, just as the cellphone in Alistair's pocket came to life. He gestured to the guards behind them, and Amber couldn't get her frozen feet to move before the dog-catcher was dropped loosely around her neck.

"Show our guest to her new quarters," Alistair said lightly, as if there weren't a gun trained at her and a noose laying on her shoulders. "My dear, I hope you will forgive my lack of hospitality in showing you myself, but I have to deal with a slight problem at the perimeter."

He disappeared down a side path, and Amber was left with the guards, who prodded her into a staggering walk towards her doom.

Chapter 20

TONY RAN.

As a tiger, he was an efficient machine of muscle and energy, and the jungle, unexpectedly, felt like home.

The jungle floor was springy, and surprisingly free of underbrush. Above him, tangled branches hid the night sky. Even with keen cat night vision, it was dark, and the drone of insects and frogs was like an ambient soundtrack to keep his pace.

His race at first was sheer adrenaline, but settled quickly into a punishing pace that ate the ground beneath him.

It was easy to follow the ridge as Scarlet had suggested, keeping to the high areas. It was steep here, and the land fell away from him on either side.

The forest thickened and the ridge began to tip downhill again.

He was just beginning to wonder exactly how long the island was when he burst out of the jungle onto a groomed lawn that made a perimeter around a tall stone wall. To one side, a lit driveway led to gates, and he immediately smelled the guards who lurked in shadows on either side.

He turned back to the edge of the jungle, fighting the tiger self who knew that Amber was behind that gate, and that she was in trouble. But training kept him in control; it didn't make sense to charge in without reconnaissance.

It took a long careful time to pace fully around the estate and return to the driveway; the compound was the size of a small town, and fully walled. There was only the one gate, the walls had broken glass and barbed wire at the top, and Tony noticed mounted cameras at several intervals. He suspected it was only darkness and luck that had kept him from being spotted when he had bolted out of the jungle, and was grateful for the natural camouflage of his tiger shape.

Tony even climbed into a tree, which groaned at his weight, to peer over the walls. The grassy perimeter meant he couldn't get close—jumping from the tree would have been impossible—but it gave him a view of the layout beyond the wall. A house was nearest the front gate, and what looked like an orchard lay to one side. Copious solar panels on most roofs suggested the source of their power. What puzzled him was the section behind the house, which was a sprawling labyrinth of squares with half-mesh roofs. It took Tony a moment to recognize that it looked like a zoo, and then everything clicked into place.

Relief flooded him; the collector was *keeping* the shifters he was capturing, not killing them, which meant Amber was *safe*.

Anger followed close on the heels of relief, because alive or not, they were keeping his mate from him, locking her in a *cage*, and Tony realized he was growling out loud.

He gave it some thought and decided, from his vantage, that the best place to scale the walls was back by the orchard. There was a natural rise in the grass at that point, making the wall a little shorter, and if he was careful, he might be able to take out the camera on his way over. There was a building just beyond that he thought he could hit with a good jump. They couldn't be expecting him, he thought. And what were the chances that someone was actually watching the monitors at that exact moment?

His tiger demanded action, and for once, Tony was in complete agreement.

He ran across the open lawn like a streak of justice, leaping for the wall. Walls meant to keep most animals out—or in—weren't going to stop a determined tiger, but it was still a stretch, and the barbed wire at the top drew blood across the pads of Tony's paws.

Tony wasn't as lucky as he'd hoped. He missed the camera, and landed with a heavy THUMP on the roof of the building beyond. Alarms immediately began to blare.

He leaped down from the building, and ran, full out, in the direction he remembered the enclosures being. If subtlety wasn't going to work, perhaps sheer force would.

Voices shouted behind him. He spun to find three black-uniformed guards. Two of them held guns, and the third had a staff that Tony recognized as a shock stick. He didn't care about them and turned in the direction that he knew Amber was, only to feel the sting of a needle in one shoulder. They were tranquilizer guns, he realized, and he was halfway across the orchard before he felt another one hit him.

The door separating the orchard from the zoo was wide open, and for a moment, Tony thought he was going to make it through—they couldn't possibly have planned their shots for a tiger's weight—when the effects of the drug hit him and his run turned into a stagger.

To his astonishment, his tiger legs were suddenly a man's, and he was crawling, naked and drunken, across the manicured grass. He didn't even realize he was lying down until a pair of stylish shoes made their way into his field of vision.

"A shame we already have a Siberian tiger," a crisp British voice said. "We don't have any use for this one."

"Could get a good price for him from the warlock," a Spanish-accented voice suggested.

"You... have... my... mate..." Tony managed to say. It didn't have the dramatic affect he intended, coming from a mouth half-stuffed with grass, and then blackness engulfed him.

Chapter 21

AMBER WALKED MEEKLY with the guards, trying not to be too obvious about looking around. The dog-catcher was lying unexpectedly loose at her shoulders, and when she glanced at the man holding the pole, he glared back and fingered a button on the handle. The other guard, walking behind her with the gun trained on her, cleared his throat, and Amber put her head down and continued to shamble with them. She was short, so it was easy to walk slowly and look like she was using a normal pace.

The looseness of the noose around her neck got her brain spinning.

They were expecting a mountain cat—an American mountain cat. A *big* mountain cat. If she shifted, the dog-catcher would be tight around the neck of a big cat. But around her small cat shape...

As quickly as the idea occurred to her, Amber put it in motion, shifting as she pretended to stumble.

Her clothing fell away from her cat form even as she jumped—straight through the noose—and scrambled for the wall of the mesh enclosure they were walking past. She heard the crackle of the dog-catcher rather than feeling it through her thick fur, and realized belatedly that it must be electrified. She wasn't sure if she would have made this attempt if she'd known that, but it was far too late now, and her coat, meant for cold mountain winters, had protected her from the worst of it.

She climbed in a panic, the agility of her cat form driving her, and as the guard behind her fired and missed, and missed again as she switched directions up the enclosure and reached the roof.

She heard the zoo erupt into roars and animal cries of encouragement. A human voice even cried out, "Go, kitty cat!"

"Shit!" the guards said in unison.

More wild shots followed her. Needles hissed by as Amber made it up to the roof of the enclosure. She ran and leaped to the next. She was already two cages away while the guards were still peering up onto the first. Then she switched directions entirely and leaped across the path to a new row of cages.

Her night sight let her see better than she had as a human, and her height gave her a clear view. Lights all along the wall had come on, showing her that she had no real chance of getting over them—though she could probably squeeze between the barbed wire with little damage thanks to her coat, she was too small to make it to the top of the wall to try; nothing was built up close to it. She noticed the cameras, too, now swiveling back into the enclosure to try to find her, and had a glimpse of a helicopter on one of the low roofs towards the back.

"Goddamn it, do you see it?" one guard called to the other.

"Beehag said it was a mountain cat, not a goddamn *little* cat!" the other complained.

Their voices were clear to Amber's excellent hearing.

Instead of immediate escape, Amber looked for hiding spaces, and found one in a pile of construction materials towards the end of the zoo. While the cameras were still re-positioning to try to follow her, she dashed out of sight down the side of one of the enclosures and flattened herself to fit in a tiny space on top of a pile of rocks, under dimension lumber and roof tiles. From here, she could see a dozen more hiding places that she'd be able to make it to in short order, and she had a good vantage for seeing oncoming intruders.

She could actually see that the entire zoo was actually much more suited for containing big animals. She'd be able to get out, she felt, with her first taste of confidence as the adrenaline began to release its hold on her. She just had to lie low, and she'd be able to sneak out of the front gates when the timing was right.

"Call it in!" one of the guards was saying.

"Fuck no, you call it in," the other protested.

Eventually, they worked out who was making the call, and the little two-way radio crackled in return as they explained their mistake.

"Escaped?" Even over the poor quality radio from a distance, Amber recognized Alistair's voice, and it made the hackles on her neck rise.

The guards fell over each other to justify their actions, and Amber gave a little cat smile to hear them describe her as basically supernatural.

There was a moment of silence in response, and then Alistair's crisp accent. "She won't get far. We've got her *mate* here."

Mate?

Amber knew without a doubt that they meant Tony, and it was everything she could do not to bolt from her hiding hole right then to find and defend him. But what did they mean by 'mate?' She could all but hear the emphasis that Alistair was putting on it.

The waiter at the resort had used the same word.

Whatever they meant by it, she knew that Alistair was right—knowing that they had Tony—that they might *hurt* Tony to get her, meant that Alistair had Amber as surely as if that noose *had* been tight around her neck.

Chapter 22

TONY CAME TO THROUGH a haze of confusion and misery. Sunlight was just beginning to peer over the high walls, and he realized he was lying in a thin pile of straw over a concrete slab with fine chicken wire over it, and it was dreadfully uncomfortable in his human form.

There were thick bars all around him, and he could see more bars overhead. A small lean-to in one corner provided some protection in case of rain. There was a shallow tub of water.

He was aware of desperate thirst, and his tongue felt oddly thick. His hands and feet had fading scratches, and he remembered the barbed wire that had scraped them on his way over the wall.

Tony...

The voice in his head was not, he felt, exactly directed at him. It was an internal lament, a cry of pain and longing and confusion.

"Amber!" He said it out loud as well as through animal speech, reaching out for her with his mind.

Her surprise and relief did not exactly have words, but felt like a tackle hug. *How are we doing this?* she asked.

Some shifters just can, Tony explained. *Where are you? Are you alright? Are you... free?*

He got an impression of crouching in a small dark place with her answer. *I'm nearby, just to the east,* she said. *I can see you, but I don't want to show myself. They haven't caught me yet.*

Get out of here, Tony told her fiercely.

I'm not leaving you, Amber insisted.

They'll use me to try to capture you, Tony told her flatly. *Better that you aren't here at all. You have to get out.*

I'm not leaving you, Amber repeated stubbornly.

Use logic! You know you can't fight them all. You can get help, at the resort.

She didn't answer for a moment, then asked, *What's a mate?*

Tony sat up gingerly. The drugs had left his limbs feeling odd and as if all the joints were too big. *You're my mate,* he told her gently, mindful of how frightened she had gotten when he called her beautiful. *You're the one other person who completes me, the one true match for my soul and body.* He couldn't help but remember her body, all curves and velvet skin against him.

Amber was quiet in his mind, contemplating. *And you know your mate at once when you meet?*

Tony nodded. *With every inch of your spirit.* At least, he had. Had she?

Her laughter was a rich caress of his mind. *I thought I was going a little crazy when we met,* she confessed.

I had never seen anything in the world as gorgeous as you, Tony told her, deeply relieved. *And I will never forgive myself if you get captured because of me.*

You got captured because of me, Amber pointed out.

Tony had no answer for that, but wordlessly pleaded that she see reason and leave while she could.

Reluctantly, she finally answered. *I'll go,* she agreed. *But only to get help. I'm coming back for you.*

Tony had a sense of her, ghosting out of her hiding place and darting from shadow to shadow, her attention entirely on staying quiet and out of sight.

He wanted to implore her to be careful, but didn't want to distract her from her stealth. Instead, he stood, cursing his wobbly legs, and shifted into a tiger to explore the cage with the extra senses that came with it. The water smelled good, so he indulged in a deep, refreshing drink.

He smelled Beehag before he saw him: Indian spices, fine wool, and just a touch of whiskey.

"Ah," the odious man said, stopping before Tony's cage. "I like it when my guests stay in animal form. Some of them have to be... convinced to do so."

Mostly to spite him, Tony shifted back into a human, and stood up to scowl through the bars, arms crossed. He was actually glad for the week at Shifting Sands; being nude felt comfortable and powerful, when a week prior to that, it might have felt like a weakness.

Beehag frowned, but didn't look surprised. "Your cooperation isn't necessary, anyway," he said with an arrogant shrug. "You aren't really my goal here." His eyes glinted as his face slid into a smug smile. "She's a pretty little thing, isn't she? And surprisingly clever."

Tony wanted to reach through the bars and take the man by the throat, but knew it would be futile. There were two men with guns flanking the billionaire, and Tony suspected that they weren't *both* loaded with tranquilizer darts by the way the second guard was holding his.

Beehag had a black plastic box in his hand, and he lifted it. "She won't get far," he promised. "She wouldn't leave her mate. Not when he was in such agony."

Tony gritted his teeth, waiting for one of them to take a shot. But Beehag simply pressed a button on his box, and electricity jolted through him.

It was impossible to stand still, and there was nowhere to escape—the energy was coursing through the floor and the bars and not even the straw was enough to keep it from burning up his feet. The shock was not strong enough to kill him, but it was bitterly, burningly painful, and Tony couldn't keep back the yell of agony or keep his muscles from convulsing. It stopped just when he felt like he couldn't take another moment, and he stared through the bars at Beehag in impotent fury, panting and clenching his fists.

The smell of singed straw filled the cage.

"Do you know what a shifter's weakness is?" Beehag asked in his silky voice. When Tony didn't reply, he went on anyway. "A shifter can't help but shift if they are in enough pain..." He lifted the box again, and although Tony was braced for it this time, he was still not ready for the piercing pain.

True to Beehag's observation, Tony shifted without meaning to. He even tried to fight it, briefly, and was disappointed to find that the pain was no less in cat form. His tiger, however, was more capable of dealing with the pain, and his human self could only whimper at the torment while his tiger roared and flung himself uselessly at the cage.

Beehag stopped the electricity at last, and Tony paced the cage in tiger form, still staggered from the experience. He was not sure he would have been able to shift back if he had wanted to, he was so shaken by the torture.

"That ought to bring her," Beehag said, deeply satisfied. Somewhere down the pens, a single wolf raised its voice in a howl of sympathy. The rest of the zoo was eerily quiet.

Chapter 23

AMBER DARTED FROM SHADOW to shadow, skittering through open drainage channels, under equipment, and across roofs, where she dared.

There was too much open space between the gates and house; she wasn't sure how to get from one to the other, or how to get through the gates once she got there. She tried to keep a map in her head, adding more to it as she noted landscapes and oddities, like the helicopter on a warehouse roof towards the back.

She nearly fell off the rain gutter when the pain began.

"Tony!" she cried, but he was too lost in agony to hear her or answer.

Beehag.

If he had been in her reach, she would have gleefully clawed his eyes out at that moment.

She nearly turned back, but she knew that the British asshole was just waiting for her. She wasn't sure what she was going to do, but it didn't involve falling into his trap like a stupid fool. It might have broken her heart to realize he was hurting Tony, but it didn't take more than a moment of rational thought to realize that he was doing it deliberately to draw her back.

It only steeled her purpose. She was going to return to the resort. She would ransack Tony's cottage—he must have secret government super-spy contacts she could reach. They probably had helicopters, or maybe squadrons of dragons. She'd tell them everything, and make them promise to send help, then come back and turn herself in to make them stop hurting him. She'd promise cooperation, if they let him be, and generally delay everything long enough for rescue to come.

When Tony's agony let up, she didn't try to contact him. She knew her will would waiver if she let herself touch his mind again.

Instead, she crept along to the front of the house, keeping to the valleys of the roof and watching for the cameras. She could hear a crash and commotion, and suspected that they were mobilizing—did they guess that she would try to escape? She expected them to be ready for her near Tony's cage; she had hoped that they would be distracted from the gates for that time.

To her surprise, the gates were open, and the beat-up van from Shifting Sands was wedged between them. Four guards with weapons—Amber had no idea if they were real ones or only tranquilizers, but wasn't willing to risk finding out the hard way—were surrounding it. They clearly looked flustered.

Jimmy was loudly protesting from the driver's seat that they were scheduled, that Mr Beehag had arranged a tour. "Just radio Mr. Beehag! I swear, he's expecting us!"

Amber's ears flattened against her head in confusion. The van was completely full of resort guests. As she watched, Magnolia made her ponderous way out of the side door, calling over one of the guards to take her imperious hand as the van tipped under her weight.

"Here, darling, stop waving that around and come help a lady down!" she commanded, and the guard actually did so, putting his hand out reluctantly to steady her.

The other resort guests weren't guests at all. Amber recognized a flash of Scarlet's distinctive hair in the passenger seat, and the person out after Magnolia was the surly gardener, who didn't so much as pretend to be friendly before punching the guard who had his hand captured in Magnolia's.

"So uncivilized," Magnolia said with a sniff as they began to brawl in earnest, but she didn't let go of the guard, demonstrating unexpected strength as he twisted and tried to break free. The gardener made short work of him, given his handicap, and Magnolia gently lowered the unconscious man to the ground after only a short flurry of blows.

Chef, out next, immediately asked if she was alright, not even giving the remaining three guards a glance.

"He didn't hurt you, did he?"

"I'm fine, sugar," Magnolia insisted, straightening her hat. "You're a dear to ask!"

Scarlet dismounted from the passenger seat like a queen, with her staff fanning out behind her as they scrambled out of the van like some kind of shifter clown car.

The remaining three guards fidgeted in place, swinging their guns from one target to another nervously. The youngest of them finally picked up their radio. "Um, sir? We've got trouble at the gate. Guests. Er... the resort lady. And... some staff, I guess. A guard is down."

"Tell Mr. Beehag that Scarlet Stanson is here to discuss some of the terms of our contract," Scarlet suggested sweetly, folding her arms and giving the guard a steely stare.

Several other guards ran up then, taking positions with partial cover and training their weapons on the motley crew. The first three took more confident stances and the young man with the radio looked back at Scarlet defiantly.

Then the last person disembarked from the van wearing a brilliant yellow lifeguard shirt, and shifted immediately into a dragon four times the size of the van. To a man, the guards all stepped back and re-positioned their hands on their guns.

The youngest guard picked up his radio again and said with a wavering voice. "Miss Scarlet is here... uh... to talk about a contract. They brought a *dragon*, sir..."

Chapter 24

ALISTAIR BEEHAG STOOD in front of Tony's cage, looking almost bored. "You know," he said, condescendingly, "It isn't really worth all this fuss. I give my guests everything they could possibly need. I assure you that Miss Allen would be quite safe here. She would even stop trying to escape, eventually; they all do."

Tony shifted back into human form, because he could again, and because as a tiger it was getting difficult to keep himself from throwing himself at the cage walls in sheer fury.

He cursed at Beehag using every expletive that Rick had ever taught him.

It wasn't as satisfying as he had hoped and Beehag only laughed.

He went on conversationally, "Some of these shifters have been here for decades," he explained. "My father collected them when he was a young man, and passed his collection to me. Did you know that shifters live as long as humans even in their animal forms exclusively? It would be a wonder to the scientific community if they got their hands on some of my guests. Amber is quite young—I imagine she will live out a very long life here."

Tony might have flung himself at the cage even in human form if the bastard had kept going on, but fortunately one of the guards' radios crackled to life.

"Um, sir? We've got trouble at the gate. Guests. Er... the resort lady. And... some staff, I guess. A guard is down."

Beehag sighed, as if it was just a little inconvenience, but there was a glint to his eyes that Tony didn't like.

With an imperious gesture, Beehag sent half of the guards scurrying to the front of the estate like ants.

The remaining guards barked orders into phones, and didn't seem the slightest bit fazed when a panicked message came over the radio: "Miss Scarlet is here... uh... to talk about a contract. She brought a *dragon*, sir..."

Far from being alarmed, Beehag actually clapped his hands. "Oh, this is a good day," he said gleefully. "I have been unsuccessful in tempting that one away from the resort since it first arrived, but I've had a cage prepared for it all this time. And I've made all the precautions for capturing it." A gesture to the remaining guards sent them scurrying.

"I hope you will forgive me for bringing our conversation to such an abrupt end," Beehag said dismissively. "I am not yet sure if I will have further need of you, but I will keep you alive until I have the mountain cat safely in hand. Until then!"

Tony did fling himself at the cage then, roaring in anger and shifting as he leaped.

Beehag only laughed as he walked away, and flipped the switch on his control one last time to deliver blistering jolts of pain into the snarling tiger.

Chapter 25

AMBER WRITHED IN COUNTERPOINT to Tony, snapping at the air as she kept herself from bolting by instinct back to the terrible zoo.

When it stopped, she lay panting for a long moment, anger clouding her vision as much as the echo of Tony's pain.

More guards were spilling out of the house, taking cover behind a waist-high wall that had appeared merely decorative, but now seemed very cleverly defensible. Several had moved out along the walls, looking poised to close in on the gate if the interlopers moved out onto the lawn.

Scarlet and her staff hung back, not entirely willing to leave the partial cover that the van provided or abandon their escape route. The staff, most of them unarmed, looked nervous, but Scarlet appeared unruffled, in her tidy business skirt and heels. The dragon roared, flaming into the air and snapping its big wings, but Amber thought it didn't look as intimidating once the shock of it had passed.

These new guards did not appear to be of the same easily-cowed stripe as the first ones, and Amber could hear them talking among themselves as weapons were passed out.

"These will turn 'em human, even the dragon," one assured another. "Aim for the bits between the big scales. Beehag wants them all tranqed because he's not sure what they are, especially the red-haired bitch."

Amber had a sinking feeling in her heart; the resort staff, plucky as they appeared, was no match for the uniformed, armored task force that faced them. There was little she could do, even behind the lines of the enemy. She was astonished by how many guards had boiled out of the estate—there must be two or three dozen men. Knowing that the guns they held were tranquilizers didn't make it any easier to take them out.

It was too bad she couldn't free the inhabitants of the zoo to fight with them.

As soon as the idea occurred to Amber, she was in motion, scrambling quietly back over the roof to the back of the house. If everyone was here, distracted by Scarlet's invasion, then there couldn't be more than a token guard back at the security room—where the locks to the cages must all be controlled.

She leaped easily down to the ground using a plumeria tree by the back door. To her frustration, it was locked. In human form, uncomfortably naked, she paced, trying to come up with some new plan, any shred of an idea.

She flitted back into cat form at the sound of officious footsteps and hid in the shadow of a big planter by the door.

Beehag.

He was smiling confidently and tapping a black box in his hands. With a lazy swipe, he used his keycard to open the door with a whir and a click.

Why wouldn't he be confident, Amber thought despairingly. He knew he had all the advantages.

Still, she wasn't going to give up yet. She held her breath, and darted in at his heels, as quiet as a whisper, pretending she was nothing more than a shadow behind him. She followed him down the corridor until they came to a closed door. Alistair swiped his card, and then put his thumb on a small screen by the security panel. The door whirred and opened with a little pop.

Amber followed him, barely getting her tail swished in behind her before the door closed with a hiss and a click. She knew she couldn't have made it in undetected if Beehag hadn't been so distracted.

One wall was a panel of screens, showing all the parts of the compound. Animals paced in dozens of cages, looking clearly agitated; they must know that something momentous was happening. Amber's eyes went immediately to search for Tony, and found several cages of tigers, one pure white and black, and two the more common orange and white and black. More screens showed the front lawn, and it was to these screens that Alistair immediately went.

Behind him, Amber's attention swung to the opposite wall, where a rack of weapons hung. She couldn't tell if they were real guns or tranquilizers, but it didn't matter to her now.

Quietly as she could, she shifted to human, standing up slowly and reaching for one of the rifles.

"Fools!" Beehag said mockingly, making her freeze in place.

But he was only talking to the guard who sat there, and the figures on the screen. A quick glance showed that Scarlet had moved away from the van and was speaking to guards, her hands up in a position of surrender. There was no sound from the screen, but Amber thought that her posture had more defiance than yield to it. She released the safety on the gun before taking it down, and a fortunate shift of a chair covered the sound.

As she suspected, actually releasing the gun was noisier, and both the guard and Alistair turned in alarm to face her as she swung it down, turned and aimed at them.

Their moment of shock gave her a chance to release a dart directly into the guard's neck, and she was gratified to see him crumple almost at once.

Alistair had an odd look of alarm and amusement, and Amber half-wished she had picked a gun with real bullets so she could wipe that smug expression off his face forever.

He put his hands up slowly. "What a clever little kitty you are," he said with an odd twist of his lips. "How did you get the resort staff mobilized? I was hoping to milk them as a source for my collection for much longer, but I knew they'd become a problem eventually. Your friend Tony just hastened that end, nosing around like he was. What I couldn't have hoped for was a chance to capture them all—I had thought they would all have to go down in the terribly *unfortunate* fire that I've already arranged."

Finger twitching on the trigger, Amber paused. "Fire?" she said.

As slowly as they'd gone up, Alistair's hands went down. "The resort is rigged," he said confidently. "Everything is in place to go up at sunset tonight. It's a shame no one will survive. But you know how unpredictable natural gas fuel can be, and construction regulations in a country like this can be a little *lax*. Besides, they're only shifters."

"You're a monster," Amber spat, thinking of all the innocent resort guests who would be killed in the tragedy.

"You're the ones who turn into *animals*," Alistair said in disgust, raking her naked body with his glance. "You have to keep me alive," he insisted. "If you want any chance of disarming..."

Amber pulled the trigger, racked the slide and fired again, sending a second dart straight into his chest beside the first.

Alistair's face twisted in anger and then went slack as he collapsed over the chair and fell to the ground as it rolled away. Amber resisted the urge to shift just so she could claw him in the face and dropped the gun to pounce at the control panel.

Chapter 26

TONY'S ROARS SUBSIDED to growls as the pain from the shock faded. His anger was not the slightest bit banked, and he gnashed his teeth.

The inhabitants of other cages were agitated, many of them up and pacing at the front of their enclosures. None of them shifted into human, or tried to communicate.

He wondered how long Alistair had spent with his box of pain, training them to stay to animal shape, and how far gone they were, trapped within their non-human forms.

He longed to reach for Amber with his mind, but feared drawing her back in to Alistair's trap. With luck, she was far, far away by now, not even aware of the commotion that had drawn Beehag away from his zoo.

When the lock at his cage did an unexpected whir-click, Tony thought he must be imagining it. He heard other clicks, all up and down the row of cages.

Then a mind brushed his own. *Tony? I think I unlocked the cages?*

You beautiful, sexy genius, he answered, shifting so he could reach through and unlatch the door. *But didn't I tell you to get out of here?*

My social worker always told me I was unreasonably defiant when I was a kid, Amber said smugly. *Guess I never grew out of it.*

Don't ever, Tony said with a mental caress. *I love you just the way you are.* He gratefully left the cage and went to the one next door.

A maned red wolf stared back at him.

"You're free," Tony said, voice pitched to carry. "You're all free!" He unlatched the wolf's door, and it circled once before tentatively stepping out onto the pavement, still in wolf form.

Down the path, a few doors unlatched, and several naked people stepped tentatively out, blinking and flexing fingers curiously. More of the animals whined and refused to shift, waiting for someone to come open their cages; Tony had to wonder if they had forgotten how to be human, or if they were still just afraid. Several of them hid in the backs of their cages and didn't come out even when the doors were opened for them. A gazelle simply fled, hooves clattering on the pavement as it bolted in a zig-zag path towards the back wall.

The red wolf changed at last, into a crouched man with blazing red hair. He stood up unsteadily, then walked with more confidence to Tony. "You have a way to get us out of here?" he growled, as if his vocal chords hadn't been used in years.

On cue, Amber appeared, rushing from the house, burdened with an armload of guns. "They're tranquilizers," she panted. "And I heard one of the goons say they turned shifters human, too. We have to go help Scarlet and her staff at the front gate if we want to get out of here."

The red wolf shifter took one, checking the chamber expertly, and several other human figures ghosted forward to take their own. A white tiger, staying in animal form, shook his head and snarled, lifting one paw and unsheathing his claws suggestively. An ocelot and a red panda circled Amber curiously, but didn't shift. The other people and animals hung back, listening.

Tony took Amber's last gun, and swept her into a bone-crunching hug. "You were supposed to get out," he repeated.

"I saw an opportunity to do more good here," Amber said with the breath she had left from his crushing embrace. It was terrifically distracting having her up against him with both of them naked, but there were more important things happening.

Because just then, shots rang out from the front of the house.

The red-haired wolf shifter pointed to the east of the house, pointed at Tony, and pointed west. Without a word, he selected a handful of the fittest humans and the white tiger, then led them around the corner of the house at an easy lope.

Tony gripped the rifle in one hand and Amber's hand in the other and they broke into a run, a ragged sea of animals and people surging with them. It was a motley crew at best, broken-spirited animals and staggering humans—almost all of them naked. Counting the red wolf's crew, there were still only eight guns, between them all, and although some of the animals were predators, many of them were not. The only thing they had on their side was the element of surprise, and Tony prayed it would be enough.

"Oh, Tony, there's more," Amber said breathlessly, as they ran. "Beehag has rigged the resort to explode! At sunset! All the poor guests!"

Tony looked at the sky—midafternoon, and it was a several hour drive from the estate to the resort. "We'd never make it in time to disarm an explosive!"

"I saw a helicopter on the roof of one of the buildings in back," Amber panted. "Can you fly one?"

Tony had to laugh, because the whole situation was beyond crazy. "Of course I can," he said with mock arrogance. "I'm a super spy, right?"

Chapter 27

THE SCENE THAT GREETED them was even more chaotic than the one Amber had left. The dragon lifeguard had returned to human form and lay in a twitching heap in a patch of burnt lawn, riddled with feathered needles.

A giant polar bear was roaring over the waist-high wall. Its motions were a little drunken, and several darts hung in its brilliant fur, but guards were still scattering before its enormous paws. Scarlet was still in human form, crouched behind most of a wooden plank thick with needles as more of them hissed into her make-shift shield. Half a dozen unconscious humans lay naked across the lawn.

It was into this bedlam that Tony charged, firing quickly at the most competent-looking guards. The sea of animals and humans that were running with him spilled out into the guards, and though their enemies' shots were true, sheer numbers sent the ragged team forward. The polar bear made it over the little wall, but collapsed onto the guards with a whine and lay still, pinning several of them as it turned into Magnolia.

Amber shifted into her cat form, figuring she would be harder to hit if she were smaller, and felt a dart ruffle her fur as she hit the ground running.

She leaped onto the nearest guard, scratching at his face and hissing.

He staggered back and shot wildly into the air before falling backwards with a dart in his shoulder.

Tony fired the last dart from his gun and Amber caught a glimpse of him shifting into tiger form before she was dodging the swung muzzle of a gun from a guard who was out of darts. She hissed, and as she crouched to leap on him, he staggered backwards with a needle in his throat.

The red wolf shifter's team had flanked the guards from the other side of the house, and the red-haired man was taking down everyone in uniform with grim, sharp-shooting precision, taking a gun from one of the others in his team when he ran out of darts.

In a matter of moments, the battlefield had stilled to growls and hisses. A grizzly bear, shaking a dart from the ruff of its neck, staggered to where the polar bear had collapsed, and changed into Chef, gingerly pulling Magnolia's head into his lap as he sank wearily down beside her.

Scarlet put down her shield and stood up, as gracefully and self-possessed as if she weren't surrounded by the knocked-out bodies of most of her staff.

The animals from the zoo milled about uncertainly, and everyone who was ambulatory gradually found themselves in a loose semicircle around the resort owner. Amber put her hand in Tony's and squeezed wearily. Most of them shifted to human, but not all. The maned red wolf drew himself forward as their spokesman. "We're obliged for your assistance," he said gruffly.

At that moment, the gazelle charged from behind the house, skittered to the side when it encountered the mass of people and animals, and then fled wildly through the gate, leaping over anything in its path and finally charging over the van with a clatter of panicked hooves.

An elderly woman buried her face in her hand and wept. "I don't know what I'll do now," she sobbed. "It's been twenty years since I saw my family."

"Some of these people have been here decades," Tony said, remembering. "Some of them may not remember how to be human."

"You have a home at the resort," Scarlet said, unexpectedly. "We can find beds and food for everyone, and the resort is as welcoming to shifters in animal form as in human." She lifted her voice to include them all. "Everyone who needs a place may stay there, until you can contact family, or as long as you need."

Amber clenched Tony's hand in her own, and as one, they said, "The resort!"

Scarlet's eyes drilled into them. "What *about* the resort?"

"Beehag," Amber said, then she explained as quickly as she could. "He says he rigged the resort to explode tonight at sundown. Tried to use it as leverage so I wouldn't shoot him."

"I hope that you did anyway?" Scarlet's voice was dry and hard.

"Twice," Amber said with remembered satisfaction, and she was rewarded by a grim nod from Scarlet.

"That's my mate," Tony said proudly.

"He said something about the natural gas," Amber remembered.

"*Jimmy*," Scarlet spat. "I caught him fooling with the hot water heaters earlier this week. He had some excuse about the settings being too high." She looked around suddenly. "Where *did* Jimmy go?"

A swift search revealed no sign of Jimmy among the unconscious on the lawn.

Tony hissed, "Beehag."

The three of them dashed for the security room at the back of the house.

The red wolf shifter remained behind to coordinate the dazed animals and secure the guards.

No one noticed the ocelot who followed them.

Chapter 28

BEEHAG WAS GONE.

Tony roared, and curled his hands in fists by his side, barely keeping himself from smashing out at the computers.

Scarlet crouched at the floor, and picked up something small. A hypodermic needle, it appeared. "A stimulant, as an anecdote to the tranquilizer?" she theorized.

"The helicopter," Amber said urgently, tugging at Tony's arm as he muttered every curse word he knew.

Scarlet looked up sharply. "There's a helicopter?"

"We could get back and you could disarm the resort," Amber said, full of hope.

Tony both loved the way her trust in him made him feel, and shuddered to think he might not be able to do as much as she thought he could.

"You can fly a helicopter?" There was that dubious tone in Scarlet's voice again—as if she doubted he could drive a car, or possibly even operate a bicycle.

"Yes," he said defensively. As long as it was one he'd flown before, so he didn't have the humiliation of having to check the manual for the location of the fuel pump controls.

Amber immediately led them out of the room and towards the back of the compound, scampering as gracefully in human form as she did as a cat. Scarlet somehow managed to walk briskly enough to keep up without sacrificing her dignity and breaking into a run. Tony loped along beside her, and they all scrambled up the rickety steps outside the warehouse to the rooftop landing pad.

It was a relief to find that was that it was a helicopter Tony had flown before, a common Bell 206, all sleek and glossy black.

It was less of a relief that the blades were already spooling up.

Jimmy was sitting on the far side, controls in hand, and Beehag was buckled in beside him, looking murderous and groggy. In his hand, pointed at them from the open cockpit, was a pistol. Tony strongly doubted that it was a tranquilizer.

If it had really been a spy movie, the words that Beehag was saying would have been something dramatic and threatening, but they were whipped away by the sound of the propellers coming to speed.

"We can't let him get away!" Amber shouted near his ear.

Tony cast about for something to stop him with, discarding the idea of throwing something into the propellers as too risky just as he realized that Beehag wasn't aiming at him, but at Amber, and that Amber was already sprinting for the helicopter as if she were going to wrestle him down with her sheer force of will.

Tony couldn't let her do that; no part of him was ready to lose Amber so soon after finding her again, and he went after her in a springing tackle, desperate to get her out of Beehag's sights. He caught her in two strides, wrapping his arms around her and rolling as he heard a heart-pounding pistol shot over the thump of the helicopter blades.

For a terrible moment that lasted far too long, he was sure he had moved too late, that she had been shot in his arms and the despair that washed over him was soul-deep and searing. Then she caught her breath, and squawked in protest. He remained atop her, knowing that Beehag would shoot again, and was surprised by a streak of motion.

Scarlet, he thought at first, but a second glance showed that Scarlet was at its tail, a steel handrail she had wrenched from the stairs in her hands as she dashed across the rooftop.

The first shape was the ocelot from the zoo, already swarming into the cockpit and launching itself, snarling, at Beehag's face. Wild shots drew Tony protectively down over Amber, who was sensibly curled beneath him this time.

When he looked up again, Scarlet was pulling an unconscious Beehag out of his straps. Jimmy, face bleeding, was weeping and holding his hands up in surrender. Shots had spiderwebbed the windshield of the helicopter, but Scarlet appeared untouched. The ocelot was staggering out of the cockpit, blood dark on one spotted flank. It walked several steps and then sat to begin grooming itself stiffly.

Tony rose, shaking his head, as Scarlet gestured at Jimmy to get out of the cockpit.

"I'll need him," he shouted at Scarlet. "He knows where the detonators are, and being with me at the resort with me, he'll have plenty of motivation to make sure they all get disarmed." The pistol was lying on the floor of the helicopter and

he checked it. "One shot left," he said. Jimmy winced and cow-
ered.

"I'll take that," Amber said over the thump of the rotors, at
his elbow. "You'll have to fly us and I can handle a gun."

"You have to stay here, where it's safer," Tony said at once.

"You saw how well that worked last time," Amber said with
a cheeky smile.

Tony couldn't help himself, but had to lean down and kiss
her before striding around for the pilot's seat while she scrambled into the back seat with a not-so-accidental clip to the side
of Jimmy's head.

Scarlet had gathered up the panting ocelot, and ducked
back to a safe distance as Tony took the helicopter up, quickly
getting used to the controls and handling. A quick glance
showed that Amber had the gun to Jimmy's head, looking a little blood-thirsty in her satisfaction.

Tony had to grin as they went aloft. She was in every way
his perfect mate.

Chapter 29

THE ISLAND BELOW THEM was an emerald jewel in an azure ocean, edged in black rock and golden-white crescents of sand. If it hadn't been for the spider-cracked windshield and the weight of the pistol in her hand, Amber might have believed that she was on the kind of tourist heli-tour she had imagined taking when she had first envisioned her tropical trip; they even got a gorgeous eyeful of a tall waterfall that cascaded into the ocean below.

She just hadn't imagined taking the tour nude, and the helicopter straps were not particularly comfortable without the additional padding of clothing.

Tony certainly looked comfortable enough, his muscles gleaming in the sunlight as he handled the controls with movie-style ease. Amber grinned. As much as he had protested being a super spy, he certainly played the role well.

Even the resort looked idyllic and perfect as they circled it. It was hard to remember that they were still in danger, everything seemed so peaceful. There were a few guests sunbathing in the late afternoon sun by the pool and on the beach, and if anyone had noticed that the staff was conspicuously missing, it hadn't raised any alarm. A few people glanced up at the helicopter, but more seemed not to notice it.

Tony came to a gentle landing at the front entrance. Amber noticed that he did not turn off the engine as he poked Jimmy out of the cockpit and followed him, taking the gun from Amber. If they failed to disarm the bombs, the two of them could escape, but Amber couldn't help but think of the guests—there weren't more than a few dozen of them, but they couldn't possibly all fit in the helicopter.

"Where are they?" Tony grilled Jimmy as they scurried, bent over, away from the noisy machine.

Jimmy, limp with defeat and clearly aware of the gun that Tony was holding, pointed. "They're at five of the tanks. They aren't large enough to destroy the entire resort, but the resulting fire probably would have done the job."

He showed them to the first, and Amber cheerfully took the gun back and stayed outside the mechanical room while Tony cautiously inspected the first device near Scarlet's office, comparing what he knew to Jimmy's cowed explanation.

Amber was not all surprised that Tony was able to disarm the thing; she was beginning to think there was nothing he could not do.

"It's a very straightforward model," Tony said with a shrug, when she commented to that effect. "Bombs are not usually as complicated—or as dangerous—as they make them out to be in the movies."

Jimmy made a noise of disgust, quickly muffled when he caught Tony's dirty sideways look. And despite what he said about the danger, Amber noticed that Tony moved very carefully with the components he removed, and was not eager to have Amber close while he did his work.

The next three were just the same, Tony having Amber stay back with Jimmy discreetly at gunpoint while he went in to do whatever arcane things with wires and explosives that he was doing. The sun was just beginning to sink towards the horizon, and Amber had to wonder how close to sunset the timers had actually been set; sunset itself was shockingly short this far into the tropics.

At the pool, they nodded to other guests who were packing up in preparation of a dinner that wasn't going to be ready. They were careful to keep the gun hidden, and Jimmy was behaving very meekly. Their odd company, and Jimmy's roughed-up face, got a few curious looks, but no one moved to stop them.

"It's not like *I* was hurting anyone," Jimmy whined, as Tony ducked into the last mechanical room, leaving Amber with a quick kiss and transferring the pistol to her.

"You *knew* what Beehag was doing," Amber reminded him. "And you were bringing him shifters that you knew he would be interested in."

"I didn't have a choice," Jimmy protested. "I had debts with the mob, and Beehag made me work for him to cover them..." He must have realized that Amber lacked any sympathy for his so-called plight, and subsided to sulky silence.

"That's the last of them," Tony said with relief, coming out of the mechanical room with the device in his hands. "If they make a movie out of this someday, I hope they use really jazzy music and up the countdown to something exciting, because this lacked drama."

Amber's attention was on Tony, not on Jimmy, nor the pistol she was holding, and she was caught utterly by surprise when the weasel shifter sprang at her, wrenched the gun from her hand, and turned it on her.

Chapter 30

TONY DIDN'T WANT TO admit to Amber exactly how dangerous what they were doing was. He downplayed the risk, but was keenly aware that the mechanical room door would not keep his mate from injury if he failed to perform his job. Fortunately, he wasn't lying about the simplicity of the task; these were very basic bombs, with a chunk of explosive, embedded detonators, and a timer. There were no deadman switches or boobytraps, and the wires could simply be clipped so the detonators could be safely removed.

Elementary.

He just had to think fixedly about the fact that he couldn't fumble the explosive, or cause too much of a static shock, and he grounded himself conscientiously, both mentally and electrically.

The last one was closer to the end of the countdown than he wanted to admit, and he breathed a sigh of relief as the wires clipped and he carefully wiggled the detonators out of the explosive material.

"That's the last of them," he said as casually as he could, coming out of the mechanical room. They were in a little alcove away from the pool, but he could hear people chatting distantly out there, as if he didn't have enough C4 in his hands to send parts of the wall and chunks of tile raining down on them. "If they make a movie out of this someday, I hope they use really jazzy music and up the countdown to something exciting, because this lacked drama."

He was just wondering if he was acting too casual, remembering Amber mocking his acting ability when they first met, when Jimmy turned on Amber and pulled the gun from her hand, using Tony as distraction.

Tony had witnessed many acts of desperate stupidity over his years as an agent, but none ranked with watching Jimmy take the pistol from Amber and try to take her hostage.

He was moving before Jimmy had even positioned the gun to her head. It took all the common sense left in him not to fling the only thing he had on hand at the scene, but considering that it would have been a chunk of C4, Tony was glad that he retained enough control to instead place it gently on the ground before he sprang for Jimmy and smashed him across the face with a fist, grabbing the gun and wrenching it away.

Jimmy crumbled before his onslaught, and Amber spun away from the action sensibly.

"How did you know I wouldn't shoot her?" Jimmy whined, putting up hands in surrender.

"There weren't any shots left in the gun," Tony told him. "I lied and banked on the fact that you wouldn't have been smart enough to count them when they were fired."

Jimmy cursed, colorfully, and Tony clipped him across the temple with the butt of the gun, knocking him out with a blow that he actually restrained.

Amber swallowed. "I guess you're a better actor than I gave you credit for," she said with a hiccup. "I believed you."

"That was what sold the deception," Tony assured her. He hadn't liked leaving her with such false protection, but he knew that as long as both of them had believed it, it would work.

Amber nudged Jimmy with a toe, drawing in a breath. The unconscious man didn't move, but Tony wasn't going to take a chance. He found a roll of duct tape on a shelf in the mechanical room, and bound his arms and ankles with more roughness than was strictly needed.

Amber helped tear off pieces of the tape, then stood back when they were finished. "You really are my white knight," she said, lifting her face to smile shakily at Tony.

Tony couldn't speak, too overwhelmed by the emotion rising in the wake of adrenaline and fear. He was suddenly, keenly aware that they were both still naked. What had become almost pedestrian was sharply important again, and he could not resist the silky velvet of her skin.

His first gentle touch raised goosebumps on her arm. His second made the breath catch in her throat, and he could see the fragile pulse at her throat quicken.

"The mechanical room has a lock," he suggested, voice husky with need. He wasn't sure how he was going to get politely back across the pool deck with the hard-on that was rising.

Amber didn't answer, only followed him into the dim room and scratched his arms lightly with her nails. Her eyes told him that she was feeling as much need and desire as he was, and he was not surprised to find that she was wet and pliable when he sent questing fingers to her folds.

"Yes," she breathed as he stroked her.

He cast about the room for a comfortable place to take her, but she was gripping him with more urgency now, and drawing him down to the floor, too consumed with her rising lust to care for comfort.

He willingly followed.

Chapter 31

AMBER FELT LIKE SHE was on a roller coaster. She had spent the day afraid for her life, for Tony's life, and for their freedom. She had never realized how important another person could be to her, and now that the danger was past, she wanted nothing more than to be close to Tony, to feel his skin against hers, to feel him inside her, to have his big shoulders under her hands.

When he touched her, it felt like her nerves were on fire. Rational thought was gone, and when he stroked her lower lips, she thought she might explode.

But it wasn't enough, she wanted him closer, more a part of her, so she reached out and cupped his big, hard erection, drawing him towards her waiting entrance.

He gasped at her fingers, and shivered in need. Amber arched up to meet him, and he responded with the same urgency and animal desire that she was feeling.

He entered her with admirable restraint—Amber could feel him holding himself back, trying to stay gentle and controlled, and she was desperate for more. She was elemental, wild, and filled with need and want.

She moaned, drawing him faster, and clawed at his muscled back, begging him wordlessly to hurry, to take her faster, harder, and when it worked more slowly than she needed, she bit him, drawing an excited yelp from him.

They rolled together on the utility room floor, colliding into a shelf with nearly disastrous results, and ended with Amber on top, straddling him. He thrust up at her hungrily, and she met his need with her own, riding him and clawing frantically. She wanted him deeper, closer, harder, and drew him into herself as if she could devour him.

He groaned, and drew her down for a kiss that completed her.

And then they were one, thrusting together in perfect sensual symmetry.

There was no thought for the hard floor or the hum of machinery, or for the trauma and stress of the frantic past day, it was only two of them, perfect mates fitted perfectly together like pieces of a puzzle. They moved together in beautiful, musical harmony, and crested into a peak of pleasure that sweated out the last of their fear and anxiety.

Afterwards, they lay together for a long moment side-by-side, panting, until the discomfort of the cold floor finally penetrated their afterglow.

Amber sat up, and felt an unexpected amount of satisfaction and soreness. "If this were a spy movie, they'd run the credits now," she said, rubbing at a spot on her shoulder that had gotten bruised.

"If this were a movie, they would have faded to black over the credits some time ago," Tony laughed with a rumble.

"Depends on the rating," Amber laughed back at him, then sobered. "What really happens now?" she asked.

Tony's eyes met hers intensely. "You're my mate," he said. "I belong with you, wherever that ends up being."

"You'd leave DC to be with me?"

Tony looked martyred. "Yes, I would even live in the Midwest with you." His voice suggested what a sacrifice he would consider this.

Amber pondered. "I've never been to the East Coast."

Tony looked hopeful. "Let me show it to you," he said. "If you hate it, we can live anywhere else."

"I hear the cherry trees in spring are quite the sight," Amber said thoughtfully. "And if I could have a garden..."

"I'll buy you a house in Maryland with an acre of land," Tony promised expansively. "You can grow anything you want."

"Talk dirty to me," Amber said, and she leaned over and kissed him, deeply. Like him, she wasn't sure it mattered where they went—as long as they were together.

Chapter 32

THE LAUNDRY ROOM WAS part of the mechanical room, and Tony found clean bathrobes in a laundry basket for them to put on. It felt distinctly odd to be covered again, after spending so much time nude by necessity.

They came out of the mechanical room to find that the guests were gathered in the bar, quite sure by now that something was up. The new bartender, a tall, muscular sandy blond with a thick Texan accent, had taken charge and was handing out drinks and snacks to the best of his ability, and he had ransacked the kitchen to provide a makeshift meal of grilled meat.

He immediately asked Tony if he knew what was happening.

"I'll... let Scarlet explain when she gets back," Tony said vaguely, not wanting to try to guess what story the owner was going to have for the events of the day.

The bartender seemed satisfied with the idea that she *would* be coming back, and went back to expertly flipping burgers and handing them out to the mystified guests.

It was hours before Scarlet finally returned, with Breck driving an overloaded Jeep at the head of a ragtag caravan of vehicles full of people and animals.

Scarlet did her best to give Tony the idea that he had handled everything completely wrong, and sent her people running for bathrobes and food.

"I could have been bartending in Las Vegas," the Texan muttered, bringing a pile of cold hamburgers from the walk-in fridge that the inhabitants of the zoo fell on as if it was ambrosia. No one offered him answers as to why Scarlet was one of the only ones still wearing clothing, or where the very confused and jumpy collection of odd shifters had come from.

"Thank you for saving the resort," Scarlet said grudgingly to Tony at last.

Tony had the grace to allow that the resort wouldn't have been at risk if he hadn't been investigating.

Scarlet raised an eyebrow at him but didn't comment further.

"What did you do with Beehag?" Tony asked.

Scarlet's face was inscrutable in the predawn light, but Tony suspected that full daylight wouldn't have revealed much more. "He didn't make it."

Amber gasped. "Did you...?"

Scarlet's look was the sort you gave hysterical people and over-enthusiastic children. "The stimulant Jimmy gave him to counteract the tranquilizers was too much for his system. He never regained consciousness. The lifeguard, Bastian, is a registered EMT, and we've already called it in to the mainland. I trust you have Jimmy? He'll be answering for that crime, among others."

Tony confirmed Jimmy's location and state of restraint.

"You didn't think he might shift out of duct tape?" Scarlet asked scathingly. She sent one of her handymen to make sure he hadn't, and to keep an eye on him.

"What about all the guards?" Amber asked. None of them were among the milling refugees.

"The cages will be serving their purpose until the authorities get there." Amber suspected it was satisfaction she was hearing in Scarlet's voice.

Scarlet turned away to answer a question about housing and was drawn back into the crowd.

"Amber? Scarlet says your name is Amber?"

Amber turned and furrowed her eyebrows at the stranger who hailed her. She was a short woman with straight brown hair that clearly hadn't been cut in years. Her brown eyes were light, almost gold in the poor light of the deck.

Amber sucked in her breath. "Yes, I'm Amber," she said.

"You're... you're a mountain cat, I saw you. An *Andean* mountain cat." Her voice was rusty, as if she hadn't spoken in years, and she winced when she walked closer to Amber, clutching at her side; blood had already stained through the white robe. She completely ignored Tony.

Amber realized, "You're the ocelot who helped us get the helicopter."

"Did you... know your father?" the woman blurted.

Amber swallowed hard. "I didn't know either of my parents," she said in a small voice.

Tears were spilling out of the woman's eyes, but she smiled radiantly. "Yes, I'm the ocelot," she confirmed hoarsely. "Your *father* was an Andean mountain cat. I never knew for sure if he got you out or not, but I told him I wasn't going to let you grow up in a cage. He didn't want to go, and I'm sure he didn't want to leave you anymore than he wanted to leave me. He must have been in danger, to leave you, and not return to me. I'm... sorry you never knew him. He was very brave."

Tony was holding her hand, keeping her up with the touch, and when Amber couldn't speak, he offered gently, "I think Amber gets that from both sides. You tipped the balance in our battle, and probably saved our lives and the resort."

Amber could finally speak. "You're my... mother?"

The woman opened her arms, and Amber fell gently into them.

"My sweet baby girl," the woman murmured, stroking her hair. "You grew up so beautiful."

Amber wept, and hugged her back too hard, making the woman gasp in pain. She garbled an apology, letting go and then squeezing the woman's shoulders more gently. She shook and laughed with the overwhelming emotion. "My mother!" She turned to grin in disbelief at Tony.

Tony drew himself up straight, suddenly the object of the woman's full attention.

"So, you're my daughter's mate," she said critically. She sniffed, looked him up and down, and then said, "You'll do. Releasing us from Beehag's prison was a good first step towards earning my favor."

"Your daughter did a lot of the hard work there," Tony suggested, earning himself a warm smile.

"Yes, you'll do," Amber's mother repeated, more confidently.

They saw her to the room that Scarlet had assigned her, and Tony completely won her heart by making her bed—the staff had not had time to set up all the rooms.

"It's lovely to be human again," she said thoughtfully, stretching her fingers. "A little odd, but I like the idea of clean sheets and a bed."

Amber left her with a long, tearful hug and went with Tony to his house—anyone who could double up had, and she had already volunteered her house for a few of the refuges. Despite the fact that the sun was already rising, and Tony was exhausted in every pore of his aching body, he was not quite ready to climb between their sheets and find sleep, and he could sense that Amber felt the same way. They made their way to the deck and sat together on the wicker loveseat.

"Is being a super spy always like this?" Amber asked, snuggling against him.

"I promise it isn't," Tony said sincerely. "Something like this means way too much paperwork. We're usually much more about donuts and meetings and Powerpoint presentations."

Amber giggled, then asked seriously, "What would I do in DC?"

"Whatever you wanted," Tony promised. "There are garden stores there, if you wanted to work. Or you could be a housewife, if you didn't."

She froze beside him. "A... housewife? That would mean I was..."

Tony groaned. "I'm doing this all backwards again," he apologized, and he leaned over and kissed her head before getting off the loveseat to kneel at her feet. "I don't have a ring, I'm sorry."

Amber stared at him, golden eyes bright in the sunrise.

Tony gathered her unresisting hand into his own. "Marry me?"

The tears that appeared in Amber's eyes made Tony fear he'd done something terribly wrong until an amazed smile bloomed on her face.

"Yes," she whispered. "Oh, yes."

Tony surged up to take her into his arms, and kissed her passionately, fingers twining into her loose hair. She kissed him back, twining her tongue with his and wrapping her strong arms around his shoulders.

"I love you," Tony said, when he could breathe again. "I will love you forever."

"I love you," she replied. "Forever."

They kissed again, slower, and deeper, and Tony knew that forever wasn't just an empty word between them, but a promise, like the sun rising over the jungle.

"I'm going to miss this place," Amber told Tony, leaning into his side with her arm wrapped around him.

"Huh," Tony said with surprise. "I am, too." He had a feeling that Shifting Sands was going to stay under his skin for longer than there was sand in his shoes... and that was probably going to be a very long time indeed.

"*Pura vida*," he said. Pure life.

A Note from Zoe Chant

THANK YOU SO MUCH FOR buying my book! I hope you enjoyed your introduction to Shifting Sands Resort and would love to know what you thought—you can leave a review at Amazon or Goodreads (I read every one, and they help other readers find me, too!) or email me at zoechante-books@gmail.com. I really enjoy hearing from my readers.

If you'd like to be emailed when I release my next book, please visit my webpage at zoechant.com and sign up for my mailing list. You can also find me on Facebook or Twitter, and you are invited to join my VIP Readers Group on Facebook!

Continue this story in Tropical Wounded Wolf (Shifting Sands Resort, book 2!) ...or keep reading for preview chapters!

The cover of *Tropical Tiger Spy* was designed by Ellen Million.

More Paranormal Romance by Zoe Chant

DANCING BEARFOOT. **(Green Valley Shifters # 1)**. A single dad from the city + his daughter's BBW teacher + a surprise snow storm = a steamy story that will melt your heart.

Bodyguard Bear. **(Protection, Inc. # 1)**. A BBW witness to a murder + the sexy bear shifter bodyguard sworn to protect her with his life + firefights and fiery passion = one hot thrill ride!

Bearista. **(Bodyguard Shifters # 1)**. A tough bear shifter bodyguard undercover in a coffee shop + a curvy barista with an adorable 5-year-old + a deadly shifter assassin = a scorching thrill ride of a romance!

Firefighter Dragon. **(Fire & Rescue Shifters # 1)**. A curvy archaeologist with the find of a lifetime + a firefighter dragon shifter battling his instincts + a priceless artifact coveted by a ruthless rival = one blazing hot romance!

Royal Guard Lion A curvy American shocked to learn that she's a lost princess + a warrior lion shifter sworn to protect her + a hidden shifter kingdom in desperate need of a leader = a sizzling romance fit for a queen!

Find many more at Zoe's Amazon page!

Zoe Chant on Audio

DANCING BEARFOOT—AUDIOBOOK - A single dad from the city + his daughter's BBW teacher + a surprise snow storm = a steamy story that will melt your heart.

Kodiak Moment—Audiobook - A workaholic wildlife photographer + a loner bear shifter + Alaskan wilderness = one warming and sensual story.

Hero Bear - Audiobook - A wounded Marine who lost his bear + a BBW physical therapist with a secret + a small town full of gossips = a hot and healing romance!

Zoe Chant, writing under other names

RAILS; A NOVEL OF TORN World by Elva Birch. License Master Bai knows better than to dream about his Head of Files, Ressa. A gritty and glamorous steampunk-flavored novel of murder, sex, unrequited love, drugs, prostitution, blackmail, and betrayal.

Laura's Wolf (**Werewolf Marines # 1**), by Lia Silver. Werewolf Marine Roy Farrell, scarred in body and mind, thinks he has no future. Curvy con artist Laura Kaplan, running from danger and her own guilt, is desperate to escape her past. Together, they have all that they need to heal. A full-length novel.

Mated to the Meerkat, by Lia Silver. Jasmine Jones, a curvy tabloid reporter, meets her match in notorious paparazzi and secret meerkat Chance Marcotte. A romantic comedy novelette.

Handcuffed to the Bear (Shifter Agents # 1), by Lauren Esker. A bear-shifter ex-mercenary and a curvy lynx shifter searching for her best friend's killer are handcuffed together and hunted in the wilderness. Can they learn to rely on each other before their pasts, and their pursuers, catch up with them? A full-length novel.

Keeping Her Pride (Ladies of the Pack # 1), by Lauren Esker. Down-and-out lioness shifter Debi Fallon never meant to fall in love with a human. Sexy architect and single dad Fletcher Briggs has his hands full with his adorable 4-year-old... who turns into a tiny, deadly snake. Can two ambitious people overcome their pride and prejudice enough to realize the only thing missing from their lives is each other?

Wolf in Sheep's Clothing, by Lauren Esker. Curvy farm girl Julie Capshaw was warned away from the wolf shifters next door, but Damon Wolfe is the motorcycle-riding, smoking hot alpha of her dreams. Can the big bad wolf and his sheep shifter find their own happy ending? A full-length novel.

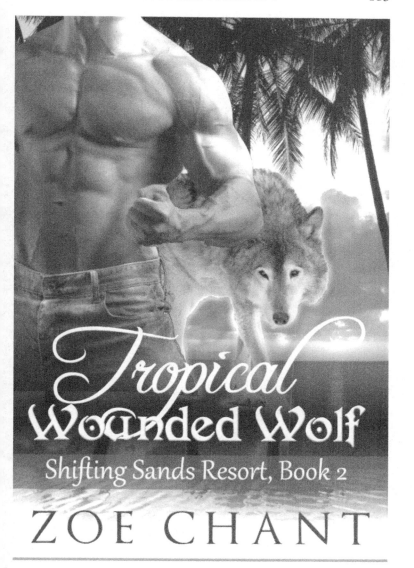

Tropical
Wounded Wolf

Shifting Sands Resort, Book 2

ZOE CHANT

Tropical Wounded Wolf

Chapter One

"I CANNOT VACATION AT a *nude* resort," Mary North said in horror. "I even have to change into my swimsuit in a toilet stall at the health club."

Her co-worker Alice, a bear shifter, rolled her eyes. "It's not nude, it's *clothing-optional*. There's a big difference, and if you're shy, you can spend the whole time in animal form."

"Oh, I don't know," Mary sighed. "The pictures are lovely, but I'm not sure I like the idea of a shifters-only resort. And it's in a foreign country, and they have poisonous snakes there, probably. Plus, two women traveling alone? We might get robbed, or kidnapped!" She shuddered dramatically, and sniffed the coffee pot cautiously. Like the deer she could shift into, Mary was wary of everything. She suspected it had been sitting out for hours on the burner.

"I'm sure they don't have poisonous snakes at a fancy all-inclusive place like Shifting Sands Resort," Alice scoffed. "And it's not like Costa Rica is some third world nation. Did you see the photo of the pool?"

"I did," Mary admitted wistfully. She loved swimming, and the brochure made the pool look amazing: huge and crystal-blue in the sparkling sunshine, with pseudo-Greek columns, waterfalls, and palm trees around it.

"And the snorkeling!"

"I couldn't swim in the *ocean*," Mary said swiftly, deciding to dump the coffee out and wait for a new pot. She had just enough time before the next block of classes to brew one.

Alice snagged a cup before she could pour all of the coffee out, but Alice lived dangerously like that.

"Have you ever been in the ocean?" Alice asked, taking a sip of the molten sludge.

"They have sharks in the ocean! And stinging jellyfish and *eels* and things. Besides, this resort sounds expensive." Mary measured the coffee grounds carefully, shaking each scoop perfectly level.

"It's not so bad, once you realize that you don't have to pay for any food, and it even includes massages and kayak rentals and guided hikes..."

"A tippy little kayak out on the ocean? You have to be kidding me!"

"... And I know you aren't spending your whole salary, living like you do. You haven't taken a vacation in years."

Mary smiled down at her second hand outfit. Alice wasn't wrong about her spending habits, and she did have a nice little nest egg put aside specifically for a vacation, someday.

Still...

"I'm not sure. It's so far away!"

"That's a great deal of its charm," Alice said dryly. "And I'll be with you, so it's not like you'd be going alone! I speak Spanish like a native, and I can protect you from eels and poisonous snakes and strange men."

"But..."

Alice shook her coffee cup threateningly at Mary. "If you don't come with me, I will undoubtedly do something reckless and regrettable, and you will have to live with the guilt of not being with me to keep me from being foolish forever."

"I can't even keep you from drinking terrible coffee," Mary said plaintively, pouring her own fresh cup as the ancient coffee pot beeped its tired announcement of completion.

Alice grinned, probably sensing her victory. "But at least you won't have the guilt of not trying hanging over your head." She drained the last of her bitter cup defiantly, just as the class warning bell rang.

Mary blew at her superior java as she gathered her teaching plan and purse. "I'll probably catch some terrible tropical disease and end up spending the entire vacation desperately ill," she predicted direly.

Chapter Two

NEAL BYRNE TURNED THE bottle of water in his hands. Even this early, the heat and humidity left a cloud of condensation on the cold surface, and he traced a pattern in it until he recognized the tattoo he was drawing and wiped it entirely out with his thumb.

That wasn't his life anymore.

He lifted his gaze and looked out over the green lawn and tropical foliage. His life now seemed equally absurd: a gazelle cropped at the grass nearby, ignoring him.

"Aren't we a pair," Neal told her.

Neal made a point of searching her out every morning, offering an anchor of humanity and familiarity from which to start her path back to civilization.

The gazelle had been imprisoned in Beehag's horrific shifter collection for longer than Neal had been there, and he had spent ten wretched years in that place. Freedom and speech still felt strange to him, and clearly the gazelle had not yet acclimated either, never shifting to her human form, barely tolerating bipedal presence at all.

Neal, by contrast, now refused his own animal form. Beehag had forced him to be a red-maned wolf in his zoo, for his entertainment. Neal rejected everything that reminded him of that captivity, burying his wolf so deeply now that he couldn't even hear its voice.

Mostly, he was ignored by the gazelle, his rusty conversation entirely one-sided, but he noticed that she came to this part of the grounds every morning, despite having the run of the island, so he continued to return, too.

"Breakfast is out," a cheerful voice announced. The gazelle moved swiftly to the far end of the lawn, ears twitching in alarm, then put her head down to graze again.

Breck, head waiter of the resort and a leopard shifter, came over to the bench where Neal sat, holding a heaped plate of food from the gourmet buffet, followed by Graham, the groundskeeper. Although the staff was allowed free rein of the resort food, they were not permitted to eat it in the guest dining room. The picnic table where Neal met the gazelle every morning had become a gathering place for a few of the staff, and somehow, despite his attempts to remain aloof, Neal had found a new place to belong in their motley ranks. He did whatever odd tasks were assigned to him, and used his free time to work at getting the remaining survivors of Beehag's prison back to their lost families.

Strangely, he could face helping them, but not the idea of returning to his own life.

Graham, a lion shifter, sat down opposite him, grunting wordlessly in what Neal now recognized was a greeting.

Breck filled any conversational space left by the surly landscaper and the quiet refugee with practiced ease. "Avoid Scarlet today," he advised needlessly.

Scarlet, the owner of the resort, had a short temper and a ferocious will. Neal knew that he and the other rescued shifters were there by her generosity and was grateful for it, but kept out of her way as much as possible. He didn't want a reminder that he and the others were costing her money to keep, and he couldn't tell her when he was going to be ready to leave the insulated island.

Breck continued despite the stony silence. "I guess there are some legal inheritance issues with the island property now that our friend Beehag is out of the picture, and there may be some uncertainty for the long-term lease of Shifting Sands," he said conversationally, eating a slice of quiche with a fork. "We're over capacity in free guests, and under in paid." He paused, giving an eloquent shrug and nod at Neal. "No one blames you, but you might want to keep out of her way, just the same."

Neal shrugged back, and Graham put an entire slice of the quiche in his mouth.

"What needs done today?" Neal asked, snagging an extra slice of the egg pie from Breck's plate over his feigned protest.

Neal hated any reminder of Scarlet's charity and avoided the dining hall whenever possible. It hadn't escaped his notice that Breck's breakfast plate had doubled in size since they first started meeting at this table, but none of them actually mentioned it out loud. Neal pretended he was stealing Breck's food, Breck pretended he was bothered by it, and Graham studiously ignored it all.

"There aren't enough guests to need any extra waitstaff," Breck answered him, picking a questionable vegetable out of his food with a fork and setting it aside.

Neal was glad. While he could feign good manners and keep from swearing, he didn't fit the dining hall any better than the waitstaff uniforms fit him.

"Always weeds," Graham growled. "And the pool needs to be scraped."

"I'll do the pool," Neal volunteered. The last time he had tried to help Graham with the gardening, he'd pulled up a domesticated vine, and he actually thought for several moments that the lion shifter was going to deck him over the mistake. He could probably hold his own against the groundskeeper, but he didn't want to find out.

After eating half of Breck's plate of food and listening the resort gossip, Neal stood up.

"I want to get the pool done before it gets too hot," he said.

"Catch you this afternoon," Breck said cheerfully.

Graham grunted.

The gazelle gave him a long soulful look from across the lawn, then wandered away through the brush.

Neal shed his resort shirt at the supply shed, and exchanged it for the long-handed algae scraper and net he would need for the pool job. It wasn't glamorous labor, but it was physically intense, and the sun on the pool deck would be brutal later in the day. It was good work, requiring attention, and Neal tackled it with all of the frustration and bitterness that boiled in his blood.

He was about halfway down the first side of the enormous pool, sweating profusely and enjoying the burn in his muscles, when he felt his red maned wolf stir suddenly, deep inside.

"*No,*" he said ferociously out loud, and he scraped at the tile more vigorously, the thin velvet of algae dissolving before his assault.

To his surprise, his wolf growled back, the urgency of his message too keen to back down.

Without wanting to, Neal looked up, and found his head swiveling to the deck by the bar.

A figure stood looking out over the bar deck, and Neal was grateful that she hadn't noticed him yet, because he had to stare for a long moment.

She was the kind of pale that only very new visitors to the resort could be, with mousy blonde hair and big, terrified eyes under a wide-brimmed hat. She had a bag clutched to her chest, and one sandal-clad foot was tucked behind the other, rubbing nervously at the opposite heel.

She had the timid, diffident body posture that usually made Neal want to roll his eyes and avoid, but there was something about her—something more than the incredibly sexy curves that she seemed be trying to hide. Something that inflamed his senses and made him acutely aware of every pore of her perfect skin.

She's ours, his wolf told him firmly, and the conviction was so deep and determined that Neal had to turn away to fight it back down.

The worst part was, Neal knew it was right. That woman—that gorgeous, petrified woman—was his mate. He unexpectedly knew the iron core of her soul, and could imagine the gentle sweetness of her mouth. He wanted to know how it tasted, more than any urge he'd ever had, and was already fantasizing the feel of her pale skin under his calloused fingers.

He drew himself up short.

There was no way in hell he was going to subject her to himself. He was too broken from his years of captivity, his control of himself was too tenuous. It would be best for everyone just to keep his distance.

He shouldered the pool tools and headed the long way around the water, to the service entrance where he would be able to avoid looking back at her. *Don't meet her eyes*, he told himself. *Don't let her see you.*

No matter how much he longed to.

The story continues in: Tropical Wounded Wolf...

Made in the USA
Monee, IL
29 April 2020